"Two weeks doesn't give me much time!"

"Time for what?" asked Daisy, looking up at him.

Adam gave her an exaggerated leer. "To entice you to me bed, me proud beauty."

"La, sir!" Daisy fluttered her lashes. "Would you trick a poor girl into a fate worse than death?"

He opened the trunk of her car and put her knapsack into it. "I'm not sure I like the idea of a fate worse than death. My previous ladies have assured me that they've enjoyed themselves enormously."

"I'm sure they did." She climbed into the driver's seat, slamming the door in a spurt of jealous irritation. "I hope you got them to write references."

"I rely on word of mouth, angel," he drawled. "And, Daisy—" she looked up from switching on the ignition "—you're lovely when you're jealous."

"Jealous. Ha! That'll be the day." She shot away, leaving him grinning.

Celia Scott, originally from England, came to Canada for a vacation and began an ''instant love affair'' with the country. She started out in acting but liked romance fiction and was encouraged to make writing it her career when her husband gave her a typewriter as a wedding present. She now finds writing infinitely more creative than acting since she gets to act out all her characters' roles, and direct, too.

Books by Celia Scott

HARLEQUIN ROMANCE
2568—SEEDS OF APRIL
2638—STARFIRE
2735—WHERE THE GODS DWELL
2831—A TALENT FOR LOVING
2945—CATCH A DREAM
2998—LOVE ON A STRING
3040—RUMOR HAS IT

Don't miss any of our special offers. Write to us at the following address for information on our newest releases.

Harlequin Reader Service
901 Fuhrmann Blvd., P.O. Box 1397, Buffalo, NY 14240
Canadian address: P.O. Box 603,
Fort Erie, Ont. L2A 5X3

GIVE ME YOUR ANSWER DO

Celia Scott

Harlequin Books

TORONTO • NEW YORK • LONDON
AMSTERDAM • PARIS • SYDNEY • HAMBURG
STOCKHOLM • ATHENS • TOKYO • MILAN

ISBN 0-373-03087-8

Harlequin Romance first edition November 1990

CHAPTER ONE

"AND YOU STILL INSIST that this is not true, do you?" said Nigel, waving the newspaper in Daisy's pale face.

"Of *course* it's not true." Daisy's hazel eyes, usually so large and luminous, narrowed. "The whole thing's a pack of lies. How many times do I have to tell you?"

"There's no need to take that tone." Nigel's expression became even more self-righteous. "This kind of thing—" he waved the offending newspaper again "—it's appalling! What about my chances of promotion? They'll never make me assistant manager at the bank now."

"I don't see why not," Daisy said. "I'm the one who's supposed to have had the affair. You can't be held responsible for my behaviour."

"But you're my fiancée. People know we're engaged," he said. "How do you think I feel? As for poor Mother... She's beside herself."

Daisy didn't doubt it. Mrs. Denton had always been convinced her only son was throwing himself away by marrying an orphan like Daisy Gordon. What background did the girl have? she'd often demanded. Daisy's father had been nothing but an uneducated market gardener, and a ne'er-do-well into the bargain—deserting Daisy's mother, so that the woman was forced to go out to work as a servant in order to keep her daughter clothed and fed. No wonder the wretched woman died young.

There had been no compassion in Mrs. Denton's voice when she made these remarks. In her opinion Nigel was simply being made a fool of by a pretty face, for no matter how much she disapproved of Daisy, she had to admit that the girl was beautiful.

"What do you think it feels like for me?" asked Daisy, her voice tight with strain. "It's no picnic having the press on my doorstep, lies spread about me and people I've known for years too embarrassed to look me in the face. As for Paul Matheson..."

Her firm lips quivered, but she made an effort to control herself. "He was like a father to me."

"Let's not drag incest into it," Nigel snapped. "It's bad enough that you were his mistress—"

"I wasn't!" cried Daisy, pushing back her tangle of red-gold hair. "I keep telling and *telling* you, Nigel! What do I have to say to convince you?" Her voice cracked. "The Mathesons were so good to me when Mum died...taking me into their home, paying for me to go to art school...."

Nigel tried looking down at her scornfully, which was difficult since they were the same height. "It's quite clear to me that when you agreed to pose for those...those studies, you went to bed with Paul," he said. "I mean it stands to reason. Why else would Mrs. Matheson make a statement like that to the press?"

Daisy felt suddenly very tired. The past twenty-four hours had been a nightmare and Nigel wasn't making it any easier. Not that she could really blame him. It must have been a nasty shock reading about the secret love affair of the village's celebrity, and seeing Daisy named as his partner. The fact that she had been seventeen at the time had added fuel to the fire of Nigel's indignation.

Daisy could remember that first horrible article practically word for word. ''Artist Paul Matheson's wife discloses that the model for his newly released canvases entitled *Studies of Marguerite* was a woman who was living with them at the time. 'My husband fell in love with her. I believe that is why the pictures are particularly good,' Mrs. Matheson declared. When asked if she harboured resentment toward the young model, the artist's wife replied, 'How can I? She clearly inspired Paul. The pictures *throb* with passion. If it took a summer affair to produce such art, who am I to object?' ''

The article had drivelled on like that for a couple of paragraphs, but Daisy hadn't needed to read it to the end to understand why Peggy had told such outrageous lies. The fact that the pictures were selling like hotcakes told her all she needed to know. When she confronted Peggy, the older woman had admitted that the whole thing was a publicity gimmick she'd thought up on the spur of the moment. But it had done Daisy no good to rage at her and demand a retraction.

''Nothing doing, sweetie,'' Peggy had declared flatly. ''Paul's sales have been slipping the past few years. He needs something like this to bring him into the spotlight again.'' Daisy had pleaded in vain, pointing out that she was not the only one who was hurt by the slander; there was her fiancé to consider.

Peggy had merely shrugged. ''He'll just have to trust you, Daisy. I'm retracting nothing.''

But clearly Nigel wasn't about to trust her. Not blessed with much imagination, and not knowing Peggy well, since he and the Mathesons had never hit it off, he accepted the published version of events.

''Why don't you go and see Peggy yourself, if you won't believe me?'' Daisy said now.

He gave her the look he reserved for customers whose cheques bounced. ''I don't see why I should have to do that. Besides, Peggy Matheson has never been particularly civil to me. She'd probably take this opportunity to—to make a joke at my expense.''

More than likely. Peggy made no bones of the fact that she considered Nigel a stuffed shirt. Pricking his self-esteem would give her immense pleasure.

The clock Daisy had inherited from her mother, along with the furniture in the little cottage, ticked loudly in the silence.

''Then there's nothing for it but to call off our engagement,'' said Daisy at last, pulling from her finger the old-fashioned peridot ring they'd found in an antique shop in Falmouth. She got a bleak satisfaction from his obvious surprise.

''Now, Daisy, don't be too hasty.''

''I don't care to remain engaged to a man who doesn't trust me,'' she said with a great deal more firmness than she was feeling. She thrust the ring into his hand. "It's the only solution, Nigel. Really."

"I didn't say I wanted to break our engagement," Nigel protested, but he put the ring into his pocket all the same.

"I won't marry a man who doesn't believe me," Daisy repeated, holding her firmly modelled chin high.

Nigel muttered, "I can't pretend to believe you, just to make you feel better."

She crossed to the door and opened it. The harbour lights had come on, illuminating the quay of the little Cornish village. It was a scene that made summer visitors camera-happy, but Daisy had grown up looking at the fishing boats moored there, and besides, she was too upset to admire the scenery. "Goodbye, Nigel," she said softly.

Seeing her determination, Nigel picked up his coat and came to the door. "You always were too impulsive," he remarked dourly. "Mother often remarked on it."

She gave him a wintry smile, a far cry from her usual radiant grin. "Then you're better off without me," she said, shutting the door firmly behind him.

She leaned against the door, shoulders drooping. She hadn't allowed herself to be bullied, and she should be feeling good about that, but she wasn't. She was feeling depressed.

She had been going out with Nigel Denton for three years, ever since she was twenty, and they'd been officially engaged for one. Surely after three years he should have faith in her. If something like this had happened to him she would have believed him. She would have stood by him no matter what others said. But the idea of Nigel being involved in any kind of scandal—no matter how innocently—was unthinkable. He was not like Daisy. Silly Daisy, who trusted people. Had trusted Paul and Peggy Matheson . . .

She felt utterly alone. The way she'd felt at fifteen when her mother died, leaving her penniless and adrift until Peggy and Paul came to her rescue.

Tears filled her eyes and she blinked them away angrily. None of that! Self-pity wouldn't get her anywhere. Action! That was what she needed. Striding across the little room she picked up the paper Nigel had left and screwed it into a ball. She was about to hurl it into the grate and set a match to it, when she had second thoughts. The way her luck was running it would probably set the chimney on fire. Better throw the disgusting thing into the dustbin. That was the best place for such libelous rubbish.

She folded the offensive article to the inside and then her eye fell on an advertisement in the travel section, headed "Need a Getaway?"

"I certainly do," Daisy muttered to herself, reading on. It seemed that the owner of a "holiday villa tucked away in the beautiful Blue Mountains of Jamaica was anxious to rent." And to rent for "a modest sum"! A London phone number was included in the ad.

She crossed the room to the phone. The receiver was lying buzzing on the table, for she'd taken it off the hook earlier when every sleazy newspaper in England seemed to be calling. She picked it up, jiggled the cradle hook for a dial tone, and started to dial.

THERE WERE HALF A DOZEN schoolgirls singing "Welcome to Jamaica" in the Kingston airport lounge. Not that there were many people to welcome. Tourists were still in short supply, for it was only six weeks since Hurricane Gilbert had torn through the island and the hotels were still picking up the pieces after its destructive rampage.

When the plane landed Daisy had noticed that the control tower was still covered with a plastic roof, like a giant shower cap, and several trees lay uprooted alongside the runway.

She had a bit of trouble with customs because Mr. Tilson Brown, the man who had rented her the villa, had advised her to take food with her; there might be shortages, he'd said vaguely. Her suitcases seemed suspiciously heavy to the stern official. But after she'd gone through every tin and packet, and assured herself that Daisy's paint box really did contain watercolours and was not a front for something more sinister, she let her go through.

Waiting for the car-rental agency to find the cable she'd sent them, Daisy studied the hand-drawn map Mr. Tilson Brown had included with his receipt for one month's rent. That rent might have seemed a "modest sum" to the likes of Mr. Tilson Brown, but it made Daisy wince. Still, she decided it was worth two years' savings, originally intended to be put toward a house for her and Nigel, to escape the relentless persistence of the gutter press.

And this...this getaway...would be good for her work. She could add to her portfolio. Maybe put together a small book. Daisy was an artist who specialized in watercolours of flowers. Just think of the abundance of tropical flowers she would be able to study while she was here, she rationalized, in order to justify her impulsive flight.

Eventually the car-rental clerk found Daisy's cable, and a small blue car was produced. Daisy, who was suffering from a combination of jet lag and tension and was ready to drop with fatigue, gasped when she left the relative cool of the airport lounge to claim the car. After the chill of an English November the heat felt like the inside of a brick kiln.

She pulled off the scarf she'd worn to disguise her long, distinctive strawberry-blond hair and threw it onto the seat. It was unlikely any reporters in this part of the world would know her, or that the story of Paul and his model mistress would have travelled this far.

Pushing up the sleeves of her T-shirt, which had seemed flimsy when she put it on that morning but now felt like a fur coat, she studied the map before setting off toward the Blue Mountains.

Driving through Kingston was a hair-raising experience. Everybody drove at breakneck speed with one hand constantly pressed on the horn. Very different from the staid way most people drove in Cornwall, and Daisy was sweating with more than the heat by the time she left the city limits.

She was particularly disconcerted by the numerous cars that swerved dangerously close to allow the male occupants a good look at her. This scrutiny was generally concluded by a flash of white teeth and a yell of appreciation. Daisy was not unused to admiration, but she found this form of appreciation unnerving.

After one ramshackle jalopy had nearly forced her off the road, she began to wonder if Mr. Tilson Brown had perhaps been right when he'd tried to dissuade her from making this trip alone. But by the time he'd discovered that she wasn't planning to bring along a friend, she'd booked her flight, paid him and made arrangements with her best friends, Marie and Peter Wilson, to keep an eye on her cottage and collect her mail.

She'd not told anyone her destination, not even the Wilsons. They were good friends, and loyal, but Daisy had discovered that even the most loyal friend was no match for the press, so she wasn't taking any chances. She wasn't spending her savings and travelling all that way to have the newspapers greet her at the airport.

When at last she left Kingston behind, the road started to climb, and became narrow, potholed and littered with rocks. She caught occasional glimpses of fallen trees, roots yawning to the sky, a legacy of the recent hurricane. A group of children, immaculately dressed in school uniforms, stared at her through enormous dark eyes and waved when she smiled at them. Three low carts, clattering on iron wheels, careered down the hill toward town, their owners sitting perilously on top of what appeared to be debris mixed with vegetables.

Then the road began to corkscrew, and the Blue Mountains appeared, thrusting their heads into the sky like a winding chain of spikes. Sometimes a car would come hurtling down toward her and she'd be forced to turn into one of the niches carved into the towering wall of rock to let it pass. But the higher she climbed the less traffic she met.

She crossed a rickety bridge spanning a swollen river, its brown waters tumbling pell-mell over rocks and fallen branches. There didn't seem to be many branches on the trees though. And instead of the dark lushness her artist's imagination had pictured, everything was a light acid green, like an English spring.

She pressed her foot down on the accelerator and the little car juddered and skidded. Maybe speed wasn't such a good idea! But the sun was sinking fast and she wanted to get to the villa before dark. She'd read that dark fell suddenly in the tropics.

When she reached the town of Newcastle, with its parade ground and plaques of ancient British regiments on its high walls, what was left of the sun was shrouded by clouds and the air was chill. She was now three thousand feet above sea level.

She stopped and consulted Mr. Tilson Brown's map again. As she drove on, the road grew rougher and the mountain crags were masked with pines. She glanced out the side window and caught her breath, for the mountain fell away from the edge of the road in a sheer drop. She could just make out the thread of the tumbling brown river and the bridge hundreds of feet below. One false turn of the wheel and over she'd go. She wouldn't look out the side window again! After a lifetime spent tramping the cliffs of Cornwall she'd thought she had a head for heights, but her Cornish hikes hadn't prepared her for the dizzying grandeur of mountains like these.

The little car strained on for a few more miles, then the road levelled out onto a small plateau. "The villa should be about here," she said aloud, for it was much lonelier than she'd expected and she needed to hear a human voice even if only her own. She was also beginning to have serious misgivings. Perhaps she'd taken the wrong road. Not that there had been much choice, but this seemed an unlikely spot for a holiday villa.

What if there was no villa? What if there was no such person as Mr. Tilson Brown? It wouldn't be the first time a gullible tourist had been tricked by a clever confidence man.

Her hands grew clammy on the steering wheel.

Then she spied the little house perched securely on a ledge above the road. There was a drive of sorts, running with water now for it had started to rain, and a newly painted sign pointed to the house. Tamarind Cottage, it read. The same name that was on her receipt.

Heaving a sigh of relief, she swung the car up the drive and skidded to a stop. Silence engulfed her, the drumming of the rain the only sound in the vastness.

Thank heaven, the key fitted the lock! There was a padlock, too, and Mr. Tilson Brown had sent her a key for it as well. "Always lock the house securely," he'd impressed on her, "even if you're only going to be away a couple of minutes. These are troublesome times."

She pushed open the front door but it was dark inside and she couldn't see a thing. Fumbling along the wall, her fingers encountered a light switch and pressed it. Nothing happened.

Blundering farther into the room, she stumbled against a low table holding a lamp and she tried that. It, too, was as dead as a doornail. "Marvellous!" she muttered.

She'd left England in a hurry, and apart from her suitcase of food had made no provisions for emergencies. There was no flashlight in her luggage, and since she didn't smoke she didn't carry matches or a lighter.

Her eyes began to get accustomed to the dark and she saw there was a half-burnt candle in a saucer on the table. Beside it lay a book of matches. They were damp and she had difficulty with them, but at last one caught and she lit the candle. The room came to shadowed life.

And a right mess it was! She hadn't been expecting flowers and baskets of fruit, but the place was dreadfully untidy. She lifted the candle higher and saw that the dining room table was covered with papers, an empty mug beside them. In the little kitchen she found dirty dishes in the sink.

It looked as if the cleaning staff, who Mr. Tilson Brown had assured her would get the place in readiness, had been camping, not cleaning. Perhaps they had misunderstood the date of her arrival, or—much more likely—once Mr. T.B. had got his paws on her money he'd forgotten to make the phone call he'd promised. She was beginning to think Mr. T.B. was full of hot air, in spite of his professed concern for her safety.

But at least there *was* a villa, and she'd arrived intact. The next most important thing was a hot bath and then some sleep. She felt as if she'd been wearing her clothes for days, and she was ready to drop.

She didn't bother unpacking her luggage, just brought it in from the car and dumped it in the first bedroom she encountered at the front of the house. She lugged her case of food into the kitchen and took out a packet of tea, some cheese and digestive biscuits. She was too tired to go to the bother of preparing herself a proper meal.

It was raining in earnest now, and black as pitch outside. It was also cold. Mr. T.B. had said it could be cool in the mountains, but he hadn't mentioned that it could be positively *frigid*. And all this rain! Wasn't Jamaica supposed to be tropical? This downpour was depressingly reminiscent of home.

There was a Calor gas stove in the kitchen, and water in the tap, thank heavens! While she waited for the kettle to boil she investigated the tiny bathroom.

A large navy towel was hanging on the rail and it was damp. Daisy was sure it had been used recently.

Bundling it into a ball, she flung it irritably into a corner and took a clean one from the linen closet.

Then she encountered another setback. Although there was a hot water tap there was no hot water. The penny dropped. Of course if there was no power for the lights, there would be no power to heat the water. A cup of tea and a wash were going to be the extent of her comforts tonight.

She hugged her arms around herself and muttered, "Welcome to Jamaica!" under her breath.

After her tea and biscuits she headed for bed. The bed wasn't made up, but there were blankets in a box and she cocooned herself in these after she'd put on her cotton pyjamas, the fisherman's sweater she'd worn when she left Cornwall and a pair of thick woolen socks. The mattress was comfortable though, and she soon warmed up and fell into a deep and dreamless sleep.

Hours or minutes later, she couldn't tell which, she was awakened by the sound of a car. Sleepily she told herself that it must be someone going on to another house higher up the mountain. Then the car's headlights shone into the room. The car had stopped outside the villa.

Wide awake, she sat up like a jack-in-the-box. Of course! The drive didn't go beyond this place. She remembered now she'd noticed that when she parked. Someone was coming *here*. She picked up her travelling clock and stared at its luminous dial.

Someone was coming here at three o'clock in the morning!

She leaped out of bed, heart hammering. She had locked the door, but had she pushed the bolts that she'd seen at the top and bottom? She couldn't remember.

The car lights went out and she heard someone moving around stealthily. A burglar? That must be it! Tamarind Cottage was being broken into!

A heavy object! She needed a heavy object to use as a weapon. Then she remembered there was a large pottery statue standing near the front door. She'd stubbed her toe on it several times during the evening.

Her mouth dry with fear, she crept into the hall, picked up the statue, which was disconcertingly light, and stationed herself behind the front door. She *hadn't* shot the bolts but it was too late now. Whoever it was had inserted a key and the door slowly opened.

Holding the statue high, she had time to register that it wasn't a gang. There only seemed to be one of them.

For an instant his dark shape loomed above her, then she brought the statue down with all the strength she could muster.

It shattered, and the man, for her intruder was male, gave a grunt of surprise and fell into the hall.

CHAPTER TWO

"OH DEAR GOD!" whispered Daisy, afraid she'd killed him.

Some tins from a bag of groceries he'd been carrying rolled around on the floor. *Groceries!* Not burglar's tools.

She turned to go back to the bedroom for the candle, but a strong male hand shot out and grasped her ankle, jerking her off her feet. The intruder rolled over and lay on top of her, pinning her wrists above her head. In the darkness she could just make out a pair of furious light-coloured eyes about three inches from hers. She hadn't killed him!

"Who the hell are you?" he rasped. "And just what the hell do you think you're doing?"

She noticed that he had a shock of untidy hair and was a muscular young man. Maybe he wasn't a burglar...maybe he was a rapist! He must have heard that the villa was being occupied by a woman alone, and he'd come up here in the dead of night intent on violation. She felt as if the blood were draining out of her body.

"You're...you're hurting me," she croaked.

"What the hell do you think you did to me?" he demanded. "To say nothing of smashing other people's property." He brought his face down even closer, and for a panic-stricken moment she wondered if he was going to kiss her. Kiss her brutally before raping her here on the floor. But he didn't kiss her. He simply screwed up his eyes and peered at her shortsightedly. "Who *are* you, for heaven's sake?"

"Never mind the introductions," she replied shakily. "What do you mean by breaking in like this?"

"Breaking in! I used my key, for pity's sake."

He had used a key. Just the same... "How do I know it isn't a skeleton key?"

"You don't. But it isn't. It's my legal key. This happens to be my house."

Her hazel eyes widened. "*Yours!* Wh-what about Mr. Tilson Brown?"

"What about him?"

"I have rented this villa from Mr. Tilson Brown for a month," she announced as grandly as she could with him lying on top of her.

"Bloody Tilly! I'll kill him," the young man exploded.

And I'll help you, thought Daisy. "And as far as I'm concerned you're an intruder. I was quite within my rights to defend myself."

"Against what? I hadn't even got in the door before you brained me."

Daisy attempted unsuccessfully to jab him with her knee. "Will you please get *off?*"

"You don't have a gun, do you?" he asked suspiciously.

"Of course not."

"All right." He rolled off. "Just don't trying making a bolt for it."

She clambered to her feet, rubbing her wrists resentfully and muttering, "Where would I bolt to, I'd like to know?"

But he stayed on the floor, scrabbling among the shards of broken pottery. "My glasses. Where are my glasses?" he demanded.

"I'll get the candle," she said, and went into the bedroom.

When she came back he was on his feet. He seemed very tall, and his shadow wavered in the candlelight in a menacing fashion. She felt a frisson of fear. Why had she admitted that she wasn't armed?

Though his voice was cultured, he looked anything but. He was unshaven and dirty, and he seemed to be covered in mud. Great gobs of it adhered to his work boots, and his jacket had a large rip in one shoulder. He looked a thoroughly rough customer, and instinctively she took a step backward. She took another one when he spoke, for he was quivering with rage.

"See what you've done?" he accused, holding out his hand. On the filthy palm lay a pair of broken glasses. "I can't see without these. Can't see to drive . . . to write . . ." he threw them violently against the wall and she gave a little gulp of terror. "You might as well have broken my arm while you were about it."

"Don't you have a spare pair?"

"This *is* my spare pair."

"Oh! I'll pay for some new ones, of course."

"Damn right you will! Presuming we can find an optician willing to do a rush job." He pulled his fingers through his hair and bits of dried mud fell onto his shoulders.

"Oh, I'm sure somebody will do it," she murmured placatingly, "when they realize it's an emergency."

"There are more urgent emergencies on this island than my glasses," he snarled, "but we'll find someone if we have to drive all day."

Feeling it was time to assert herself, she said firmly, "I'm not driving anywhere. I've only just arrived."

He began picking up the tins of food and replacing them in the paper bag he'd been carrying. "And how exactly do you expect me to drive into Kingston without glasses?" he inquired with elaborate articulation. "I wouldn't be able to see a landslide if it fell on top of me."

Her delicate brows rose. "A *landslide*?"

"They're increasing. I spent today helping to clear a blocked road farther up the mountain."

That would account for the mud and for his filthy hands and clothes. At least he wasn't a tramp. She supposed she should be grateful for small mercies.

He headed for the kitchen, cradling his bag of provisions. "I'm going to heat some water for a wash, then I'm hitting the sack." His eyes glittered in the candlelight. She wouldn't have been surprised if they had been red, like a demon's. "First thing in the morning we're driving into Kingston."

It was 3:30 a.m. and she was much too tired to argue, so she pulled her sweater down farther over her slim hips and said frostily, "We'll discuss it in the morning."

Back in her bedroom she discovered that there was no lock on the door and she jammed a chair under the handle, hoping it would hold if he decided to make a nuisance of himself.

In spite of her anxiety she fell asleep the minute her head touched the pillow. But it seemed she'd slept only half an hour when he was pounding on her door, roaring, "Come on, time to get up! Do you plan to sleep all day?"

The way she felt she wouldn't have minded. Her eyes were gritty with fatigue and her head was muzzy. What time was it anyway? Blearily she looked at her clock. Seven-thirty! She'd had only four hours' sleep. No wonder she felt like death warmed over.

The pounding resumed and she yelled irritably, "I'm *coming*. I'm coming. Stop that hammering."

She fumbled through her case for her dressing gown. It was too warm this morning for the sweater, and her cotton pyjamas were a little too scanty for comfort.

Glancing out the window, she noticed that the weather had cleared. The sun sparkled on the rolling pinewoods that rose rank on rank before her.

"Hurry *up*!" roared the bad-tempered male voice. "We haven't got all day."

Swearing under her breath, Daisy picked up her sponge bag and pulled the chair away from the door handle. Her unwelcome visitor was standing outside, naked to the waist and glaring. She registered a pair of nice wide shoulders, and a light mat of curly brown hair on his chest. The hair on his head was brown, too, and fell in an untidy swath over his broad brow. If she hadn't felt such antagonism toward him she would have readily admitted that he was attractive, although older than she'd imagined last night. Early thirties, she guessed.

Old enough to have developed an evil temper, for he was scowling at her through a pair of gray eyes that glinted nastily. Daisy wasn't used to men looking at her this way, and she didn't like it.

She pulled the sash tighter around her waist. "How do I get hot water for a bath?"

"You don't," he replied, looking at her with disgust. "Not unless you're willing to spend the morning heating kettles, and there's neither the time nor the water for that."

Hoping that hauteur might serve her better than waspishness, she said grandly, "I was assured by Mr. Tilson Brown that the villa was provided with hot water."

He bared his teeth in what could only be described as a mirthless grin. "More fool you for believing him. There's no electricity on this part of the island—and precious little water. We've had a hurricane, in case you didn't know."

She snapped, "Of course I know. I do read the papers." This reminded her of her own reasons for being here, and her pale cheeks flushed.

"Well, if you'd read them a little more closely you might have realized that a holiday in the Blue Mountains wasn't the greatest idea in the world," he said tersely.

Which was, of course, why Mr. T.B. wasn't vacationing here. He hadn't even mentioned the recent hurricane, and in her anxiety to get away she'd forgotten about it. A quick escape had been all that she cared about; she'd never thought to wonder why Tamarind Cottage was such a bargain. Mind you, now that she'd seen the place, she wasn't so sure that it was.

"Which reminds me," her unwelcome intruder continued, "I need some sort of proof that Tilly did sublet this place to you."

That was no problem, and wordlessly she went into her room and fetched Mr. Tilson Brown's receipt.

"This is no good to me until I get my glasses repaired," he said, taking the paper and peering at it myopically.

"Well, there's his name and there's mine," she said, stabbing at the receipt impatiently. She had to lean close to him to do that, and she became aware of the nice male smell of him, and the crisp brown hair on his chest...and for the first time she registered that all he was wearing was that navy towel tucked tightly around his waist. One false move and she was going to be treated to a male striptease.

"Daisy Gordon. That's me," she said, taking a step back. She prayed that when he could see the receipt for himself he'd take the initial M to mean Ms, and not put two and two together.

"Miss or Mrs.?" He hitched at the slipping towel.

"Miss. What about you? I mean," she added hastily, "What's your name? Tilson Brown, too?"

"No! Tilly's my tenant. At least he was until he started subletting without permission. I'm Adam Deverell."

"I'll need some proof that you really do own this place," she told him.

He nodded. "I'll take you in to see my bank manager in Kingston. He'll vouch for me."

"I suppose we *have* to go into Kingston." The very thought of that hideous mountain road made her mouth go dry.

"There's hot water in the kettle," he said crisply. "Be ready in fifteen minutes."

"We'll take my Jeep," he informed her fifteen minutes later, when she had swallowed half a mug of tea and washed in about an inch of water. "You do drive a stick shift, I suppose?"

Glaring balefully at the mud-encrusted vehicle, she climbed into the driver's seat. She'd dragged on the first garments that had come to hand, a pair of white linen trousers and a green-and-white-striped shirt. Some mud immediately got itself onto her trousers. Cursing, she looked into the rearview mirror to tie a shocking-pink cotton square over her giveaway hair.

"For God's sake get a move on!" Adam Deverell rasped. "We're not going to a fashion show."

"Just getting tidy," she said with maddening deliberation, tucking in a loose strand of hair. She had no intention of parading through Kingston with her distinctive hair flowing around her shoulders. There were tourists in Kingston, and possibly up-to-date British newspapers. There was an outside chance she might be recognized, and she didn't intend to risk it.

The drive down the mountain road wasn't much better than the drive up, but at least this time when she met any cars coming the other way they drew aside for the Jeep. They also shouted greetings to her surly companion, who acknowledged them dourly. Perhaps he had been telling the truth and he was the owner of the villa. If so, the next problem was how to persuade him to let her stay.

She stole a glance at his set face. It wasn't encouraging. His jaw jutted like the prow of a ship. She'd seldom viewed a more intractable expression on a human face.

In Kingston, traffic whirled about them with dizzying speed. She narrowly missed hitting a bus with a sign saying, "Hallelujah, Good Times Coming!" The passengers shouted and made encouraging gestures. At least she hoped they were encouraging.

"Here," said Adam, pointing to an optician's sign. By a miracle there was a parking space outside the building and she backed expertly into it. She sensed he was unwillingly impressed by her skill. She was mildly impressed herself. Parking had never been one of her skills.

While he was in the shop she waited in the Jeep. Taking her sketch pad and a pencil out of her shoulder bag, she started to draw a few quick sketches. A tall woman carrying her leather shopping bag on her head. A man with his hair wound up in a high narrow cone, like the stick on a toffee apple. A little boy in spotless rags, trying without much luck to sell balls of steel wool to the passersby.

Adam came out of the shop. "You're in luck," he said. "My glasses will be ready in two hours." He drew his thick brows together in a frown, trying to see what she was drawing, and she closed her sketchbook with a snap. Her drawings were none of his damn business!

"You're the lucky one," she said, putting the pad back in her bag. "You're the one who needs them."

"You don't seem to realize that you've had a narrow escape," he said thinly. "I haven't hit a woman since I was in the nursery, though heaven knows I've had provocation. But if I'd been forced to stagger around without my glasses much longer, I would have been sorely tempted."

She said, "Just remember, I can defend myself."

He gave an unexpected grin. "You're out of ammunition. There was only one statue at the villa."

He had nice crinkles around his eyes when he grinned. Just the same, she refused to be beguiled, and she asked peremptorily, "Do you want me to drive you anywhere else?"

"No. Let's leave the Jeep where it is. We're not likely to find another parking spot so easily."

"Then if you could point me in the direction of a bank I'll cash some traveller's cheques while I'm in town and meet you back here in two hours," she said, climbing out of the Jeep.

"Don't be in such a hurry," he said. "I thought you wanted to get my identity verified, or some such rubbish."

She glared at him. "I certainly need more than your word."

"My bank's just around the corner." He grabbed her elbow and started steering her through the jostling crowd. "You can cash your cheques and get me sorted out at the same time."

She tried to wriggle her elbow out of his grasp, but he did not let her go until they entered an unimposing little bank some blocks farther down the street.

"Is Russel free to see us?" Adam asked the pretty Jamaican teller.

The young woman gave Daisy a brief hard stare, then smiled brilliantly at him. "He's always free to see you." She dropped her voice to an intimate purr. "I hear you've been doin' great things to help out in Devil's Gully, Adam."

"No more than anyone else," he told her.

"That's not the way I hear it. We all think you're great." She batted her lashes. "Me 'specially."

"That's nice," he said vaguely. "Come on!" he snapped at Daisy, who was rubbing her elbow to get the blood flowing again.

He knocked at a door labelled Manager and stalked in, and she quickly followed him into a small, extremely untidy office. Seated behind a littered desk was a coffee-colored giant, who rose to his feet when they came in.

Adam introduced him briefly. "This is my bank manager, Russel Hurst."

The big man inclined his head. He must have been six foot four, and was as wide as a building. But although Adam was neither as tall nor as broad as Russel, he was by no means dwarfed by him. If anything his trim muscularity made this friendly giant appear clumsy.

"Russel, will you please tell Miss Gordon who I am," he demanded.

A wide grin split Russel Hurst's good-natured face. "Don't you know?"

"I'm serious," Adam insisted. "I need someone to identify me."

"You don't say." Russel grinned wider. "Who is this lady, anyway? Did you just pull her in off the street? Not that I'd blame you," he added. "It's a long time since I've seen such a pretty woman."

Adam ignored this pleasantry. "There's been a mix-up. My tenant sublet the villa to Miss Gordon without permission. I need someone *reliable*—" he glared a warning at the grinning Russel "—to assure Miss Gordon that I'm who I say I am, and that I have every right to ask her to move out."

Russel Hurst swept a pile of file folders off a chair and offered it to Daisy. "Why does she have to move out?" he inquired serenely. "There's room in the villa, isn't there?"

Adam fixed him with a stony stare. "I did not come here to discuss accommodations. I simply want you to tell Miss Gordon that I am the owner of the villa."

"Sure you are, man." Then he addressed Daisy. "Adam's from an old Jamaican family. They've been here for generations."

"I don't care if they've been here since the flood," Daisy replied sweetly. "I booked Tamarind Cottage in good faith and I'm staying there."

"See what I mean?" Adam said to his friend. "Another pigheaded, stubborn woman in my life. As if I haven't got enough to worry about at the moment."

Russel grew serious. "I was mighty sorry to hear that the damage at Solitaire Farm is worse than you thought at first."

"Much worse," said Adam grimly. "The root systems have been affected on more than half the trees we had thought survived. It looks as if we've lost another twenty percent of the current coffee crop."

"I'm real sorry," Russel said. "Are you goin' to cable your dad to come back?"

"What for? There's nothing he can do. He might as well enjoy his trip. He can worry about the extra damage when he gets back."

Russel turned to Daisy. "You sure chose a bad time to take a vacation in Jamaica," he said. "The island isn't looking its best right now."

"It's not a vacation," she explained cautiously. "I'm an artist. I want to paint some of your local flowers."

"There *aren't* any bloody flowers," exploded Adam. "They were all blown away."

Russel interjected hurriedly. "There might be some near Falmouth. I hear that part wasn't hit so badly."

Adam's face cleared. "You're right. Louise told me that her tulip tree hardly lost a blossom. We'll look for a hotel for you in Falmouth," he said to Daisy.

"I don't want to go to a hotel," she said belligerently.

"And how *are* the girls, Adam?" Russel put in smoothly.

"Flourishing." Adam pulled a face. "It would take more than Hurricane Gilbert to get them down."

The bank manager laughed. "Yeah! Louise was in a while back. She said the girls were sorry when it was over."

"Monsters," said Adam, a certain pride in his voice. "They should all have been drowned at birth, like kittens."

Daisy, who was getting irritated by all this chat, inquired about cashing some traveller's cheques.

"No problem! Shirley in the front will see to it," said Russel. So she left them chatting and went out to the teller, Shirley.

While she was counting her Jamaican dollars Adam came out of the office. He looked at his watch, a workmanlike affair moulded into a black plastic strap. "It's nearly noon," he said. "Be back at the car by two." He strode out of the bank, seemingly unaware of Shirley's come-hither smile.

"Ill-mannered pig!" muttered Daisy, closing her shoulder bag with a snap.

"You not one of Adam's girl friends?" Shirley asked.

"I am *not*!" said Daisy, putting on a pair of enormous sunglasses.

"Didn't think so." Her speech slipped deeper into the pleasant singsong intonations of Jamaica. "He not usually so *renk* with his women."

"I don't know what *renk* means," Daisy told her, "but if it's an insult I agree wholeheartedly."

Shirley looked at her critically. "Somethin' must have upset him. He's usually charmin'. The most charmin' man in Jamaica."

"You could have fooled me." The misguided Shirley seemed to think Mr. High-and-mighty Deverell was the best thing since sliced bread. However, *she* hadn't spent the past few hours being gratuitously insulted by him. Hitching her bag securely onto her shoulder, Daisy thanked Shirley, and left the bank.

Outside, the heat was oppressive. The scarf tied around her head didn't help. Her hair stuck to her scalp under this protective covering as if it were glued there, and she could feel trickles of perspiration running down between her breasts. Visions of palm-fringed beaches and cool swimming pools danced before her eyes. If only there had been the promise of a refreshing bath to look forward to when they returned to Tamarind Cottage, but she knew she would be lucky if she got more than a couple of ounces of water to wash off the accumulated grime of days.

Her stomach rumbled, reminding her that she hadn't eaten properly for a while, either. She must find a restaurant before she passed out from a combination of heat and malnutrition.

Looking down the street she spied a sign that read Devon House, and at that moment some tourists carrying paper bags came out of its gates. It didn't seem to be a private house.

She crossed the street, a hazardous undertaking, and went into the grounds. It was quieter inside the thick walls, and cooler, too, in the patches of shade. Groups of people were sitting at tables under a pink-and-white-striped awning, and a waiter, balancing a tray of food, made his way to the table nearest her.

Heaven be praised, the place was a restaurant! Her stomach gave another large rumble, reminding her again how hungry she was. But relief was not yet in sight, for she was told that all the tables were taken.

Assured that she could be seated in ten minutes, and since the sight of food was beginning to make her drool, she decided to browse in the little boutiques set up in what must have originally been the storerooms around the grassy courtyard.

There was a pottery shop, and a shop for Island linens. A gift shop that specialized in all shapes and sizes of boxes, hand-painted and smelling deliciously of exotic woods, and a dress shop with clever, wickedly expensive, Jamaican designed clothes. There was also a shop that sold postcards and magazines, and Daisy wound up in there to kill time and take her mind off her empty stomach.

She leafed through a tourist guidebook, and then picked up the latest copy of a popular international magazine.

There seemed to be the usual crises in the world news section and the usual flip reviews of films. She turned to the arts section and gasped aloud in shock.

Two people turned to stare at her in surprise, and she turned away to examine with mounting horror the full-page picture of herself wearing little more than a thoughtful smile.

CHAPTER THREE

IT WAS ONE OF PAUL'S *Studies of Marguerite*. He had posed her with her back to the artist, looking over one shoulder. She remembered it had been a devil of a pose to hold. A drape of white satin was lying around her hips, but her back and buttocks were naked. Her skin looked as translucent as pearls, and so skillfully painted that it seemed it would be warm to the touch. Her amazing red-gold hair fell forward over one hazel eye, and Paul had somehow managed to suggest a mixture of virginal innocence and languorous provocation. The likeness was startling. No one seeing this picture could fail to recognize her. She slapped the magazine shut, paid for a copy and headed back to the restaurant.

Settled at a corner table she ordered a lobster patty and furtively read the article. Headed ''Marguerite, Where Are You?'' it was worse than she'd feared. The journalist appeared to have interviewed the entire population of Trebethwick Cove. No one had yet unearthed Mr. Tilson Brown, thank heaven, nor discovered where it was Marguerite had flown to. But the general impression was one of guilty flight. And worse, it brought the whole dismal lie back into public focus.

There were additional pictures from the exhibition, plus a photograph of her with Paul, taken at a Christmas party when she was eighteen. There was also a picture of Nigel, taken by the magazine photographer. He looked maddeningly tragic. With growing indignation she read that Nigel was making it public that he was willing to forgive her for her past transgressions. "I realize that she was young and foolish," he'd apparently told the reporter. "She lacked a firm hand to guide her." *His* firm hand presumably!

She flung the magazine aside and started to eat her patty. It was delicious, but it might as well have been a boiled sock for all the enjoyment she got out of it. How *dare* Nigel! She noticed that he hadn't mentioned that she had broken off their engagement. He appeared to have disregarded that little item.

She took a sip of pineapple juice and tried to bring her mind back into focus and think things through. Surely public interest in such a trivial matter couldn't be maintained much longer. There must be more important things to write about than an alleged affair that was supposed to have taken place six years before. She'd just have to lie low and wait.

Then she remembered Adam's threat to move her to a hotel. But that was out of the question! Hotels contained people, and people read magazines. She might bundle herself up in scarves like an Egyptian mummy, but sooner or later she would be recognized and the press would have another field day at her expense.

She pushed aside the rest of her patty. She couldn't swallow another thing. She saw now that she should never have left Trebethwick like that. How naive not to see that stealing away like a thief in the night was bound to add fuel to the fire of scandal, not quench it. She couldn't risk going to a hotel. She *wouldn't*. And how was she going to reason with a man like Adam Deverell? A man she was sure was as unmovable as a rock once he set his mind to something. She didn't trust him enough to tell him the truth and fling herself on what little mercy he might possess.

She glanced at her watch. Hell's bells! She was going to be late. Not a good idea if she intended to try to charm him into letting her stay on at the villa. She paid her bill and ran all the way back to the Jeep.

He was sitting in the driver's seat, tapping impatient fingers on the wheel.

"It's only just two, isn't it?" She tried giving him a bright smile.

"Two minutes past," he grunted. He was now wearing a pair of dark horn-rimmed glasses and he looked down at her, seeing her clearly for the first time.

Please God, she prayed, *don't let him recognize me.*

It seemed her prayer was answered, for he said casually, "I've booked you into a hotel at Falmouth, so let's get going. We'll pick up your stuff, and then I'll drive ahead of you part of the way. I know a shortcut."

She had been climbing into the Jeep as he made this pronouncement. Now she climbed back onto the pavement. *"No!"*

He looked at her in surprise.

"I won't go to Falmouth," she said frantically, "I won't stay in a hotel...."

"If you're worried about money, forget it. I'll reimburse you the money you gave Tilly—"

"It has nothing to do with money."

"And pay for any extra expenses you might run into—"

"It has nothing to do with *money*, I tell you." She could feel herself losing control, but she didn't care. This was a crisis. This was no time to worry about charming him. "Can't I get it through your thick skull! I will *not* stay in Falmouth, or anywhere else. It's not my fault there's been a mix-up about the villa, and I'm not moving."

"But *I'm* staying there, and I don't want a woman around the place." His jaw protruded mulishly.

"I don't care what you want, you male chauvinist pig," she shrieked, hardly aware that several delighted locals had stopped to listen. "I will not be pushed off into a hotel. A hotel full of people." She looked at him wildly, "I ... I can't."

"What do you mean, 'you can't'?"

"You tell him, darlin'," a large lady encouraged.

"I ... I'm ill."

He looked sceptical. "You look perfectly healthy to me."

She clutched at her headscarf, which was in danger of slipping off. "Not physically ill."

"You mean you're mentally deranged?" He gave an impatient shrug. "I can believe that."

"Don't you let her bamboozle you, man," advised a disreputable-looking character with dreadlocks to his waist.

Daisy became conscious of the audience. For a girl who didn't want to draw attention to herself she didn't seem to be doing a very good job. She leaned forward into the Jeep, her shirt pulling tight against her firm breasts. "I c-can't take crowds," she said, "not at the moment. If I go to a hotel I'll . . . I'll fall apart." Tentatively she put her hand on his. "Please, Adam."

He looked into big hazel eyes, which were swimming with tears. She didn't usually burst into tears like this, but she was overtired, and the strain of the past week, and her broken engagement, were taking their toll.

"Don't blub, for God's sake," he commanded. A tear slid down her pale cheek. "All right. You can stay on at the villa for a few days."

"Thank you," gulped Daisy.

"A few *days*," he repeated sternly. "To give you time to pull yourself together."

"Of course," she agreed submissively. A few days would surely give her time to think of something.

"Hey, hey, she got you, man!" the dreadlocked character called, and Adam yanked her into the Jeep and switched on the ignition.

They took off at high speed, and he yelled to her over the roar, "Remember, you may have won the battle, but you haven't won the war."

"I know." She nodded, her busy mind already plotting new strategies to outwit him.

They didn't talk after that. Speech wouldn't have been possible anyway because Adam drove up that twisting mountain road as if all the devils in hell were after them, forcing Daisy to cling to the side of the Jeep, her eyes shut tight.

She only relaxed her grip and allowed her eyes to open cautiously when he slowed down to turn onto a steep track that made the Jeep strain like an overloaded mule. Then the ground levelled out and a house came into view and Daisy exclaimed, "Ooooh!" because even with only half a roof, it was the loveliest house she'd ever seen.

"What is this place?" she asked him.

"Solitaire Farm. My father's coffee plantation."

He parked by the front door. The cobbled sweep of drive was quite tidy, but a pile of broken branches was stacked against the side of the house, and now she could see that some of the upper windowpanes were missing. Two men, machetes hanging from their waists, were piling fallen rocks against the retaining wall along the edge of the garden.

"It's beautiful," Daisy said.

"You should have seen it six weeks ago. It was a wreck." Adam snorted. He jumped down from the Jeep. "Do you want to come in? You can have a cold drink while I phone."

She clambered down and joined him at the front door. "The phone's working then?"

"It has been for a couple of weeks. I want to cancel your room at the hotel."

"Oh, yes! Of course." He held the door open and she entered the hall. Inside it was all cool shadows and muted sunshine, which was marvellous after the dusty heat. The walls were freshly plastered, and the floor, which was made of a handsome dark wood, smelled of polish.

An ancient Jamaican woman wearing a loose cotton dress, a pink and yellow head tie over her grizzled head, came out of the interior of the house. "Where you bin, Adam?" she demanded. "Louise, she bin callin' for you on the phone. Says it's important."

Adam's jaw tightened. "Wants to tell me how to run things, does she?"

The old woman shook her head. "You two, you drive me crazy."

"You should be used to it by now, Lilly," Adam said with a smile.

But the old woman simply muttered, "Never get used to squabblin'."

"Never mind about Louise." He pulled Daisy forward. "This is Miss Daisy Gordon. She's visiting Jamaica, and she needs a cool drink while I make a couple of phone calls."

Lilly examined Daisy closely. "Funny time to be visitin' Jamaica," she commented.

"Miss Gordon's a funny girl," said Adam. He told Daisy, "You go with Lilly. I won't be long."

"Best come along to the kitchen," said Lilly, lead-ing the way with reluctance. "The roof's on there."

Daisy murmured, "Thank you," and hurried after the spry old lady.

She noticed that there were a lot of pictures leaning against the walls, waiting to be rehung. In fact the whole atmosphere of the house was one of drastic re-decoration. Furniture was covered with plastic sheet-ing. The windowframes were freshly painted, and she could hear distant bangings and thumpings in the direction of the roof. Clearly Solitaire Farm had been undergoing extensive repairs for the past six weeks.

Lilly opened the door and they entered a large, square kitchen. Sunshine glinted off polished taps, saucepans glittered, and the red-tiled floor gleamed with fresh wax. A young woman, who was stirring something in a pot on the stove, something that smelt delicious, turned to greet them.

"Some fruit juice for this lady," Lilly com-manded, then she gave Daisy a hard look. "Or would you be wantin' rum?"

"Fruit juice will be fine, thank you."

Lilly nodded dourly. "I'll leave you with Sarah then," she said. "I got things to say to Adam."

"We only got orange juice," Sarah told her when they were alone. "Will that be all right?"

"Orange juice will be just fine."

The girl smiled warmly, and Daisy started to relax. After Lilly's suspicious severity any sign of accep-tance was welcome.

"The oranges came from Miss Amy's farm," said Sarah, "so it's nice an' fresh."

Not having the foggiest idea who Miss Amy was but assuming that her farm must also be on the island, Daisy asked, "Didn't the hurricane destroy her trees then?"

"Hurricanes is funny things. Ol' Gilbert, he didn't hurt Miss Amy's trees too much." Her smile grew wider. "He wouldn't *dare*. 'Sides, them orange trees is stubby. Gilbert, he blowed right over top of 'em."

She put a tall glass on the scrubbed wooden table and went to an enormous refrigerator for a frosty jug of juice. Daisy sat down while the girl poured her a generous glassful.

"Won't you have one?" Daisy suggested.

"Maybe I will," said Sarah, getting another glass. After she'd helped herself she stood leaning against the kitchen counter, eyeing Daisy speculatively. "You visitin' the family?"

"The Deverells?" Daisy pulled off her scarf and shook her hair free. "No. I don't know them."

"I wondered," said Sarah. "I mean it would be a bad time. 'Part from the hurricane, Mister Deverell is visitin' his eldest daughter in Australia. That's how he missed Gilbert an' all the mess."

"I must say this place doesn't look too bad now," said Daisy. She took a sip of the ice-cold juice. "Even your refrigerator's working."

"That's 'cause Mr. Deverell put in his own generator long time ago," Sarah told her. "An' Mr. Adam's been workin' day an' night to fix up the house. Got done faster than most. That's 'cause houses is Mr. Adam's business.''

"Does he build them, then?" asked Daisy.

Sarah giggled. "Not really. He designs 'em. He's an architect.''

So that was what he did. When he wasn't helping to clear landslides, or fixing his father's roof. She wondered if there was enough work for an architect on the island. Somehow she'd only thought of Jamaica in terms of farming . . . and the tourist trade, of course.

"My family live in Devil's Gully," Sarah went on, "an' ol' Gilbert, he knocked down their house. Mr. Adam, he helped them build another one. A *strong* one this time." Her eyes glowed with affection. "That Mr. Adam, he really *somethin'*.''

"I'm sure," said Daisy primly. She could understand the girl's gratitude, but was unable to respond to this accolade with enthusiasm.

"I mean, he could have been fixin' up his beach house," Sarah explained. "It's really a mess. He still can't live there. He been stayin' in Tamarind Cottage all this time.''

Daisy said bitterly, "I know."

Sarah nattered on in her lazy drawl, telling about the storm, and how she and Lilly had scurried around, pushing furniture into dry spaces, desperately searching for containers to catch the ever-increasing leaks from the roof. But Daisy listened with only half an ear, her mind busy digesting this information about Adam.

How many houses did the man own, she wondered irritably. And if he had another house why didn't he move into it and leave the villa to her? Why didn't he move in *here*, for that matter? Daisy didn't believe half a roof would put him off. Adam looked as touch as old leather.

They heard voices, and Adam came into the kitchen, Lilly close on his heels. Sarah straightened up guiltily.

"You finished that ironin'?" Lilly asked her sharply. "Mr. Adam needs his shirts."

Sarah mumbled, "I'll do them now," and slipped into a small room off the kitchen.

"That girl!" Lilly muttered, and Daisy was sure the old woman blamed her for wasting Sarah's time.

Adam said, "Lilly tells me that the water was delivered here this morning."

Daisy opened her tawny eyes wide. *"Delivered?"*

"We have to buy fresh water to fill our water tanks," he said. "Since Gilbert it's very expensive. The going rate right now is twenty dollars a bucket, but I think we could manage a small bath. If you'd like one."

"Oh, *please*!" said Daisy, fervently grabbing at this chance to get clean at last.

"But no wallowing in a full tub," he warned.

"I never wallow."

"*All* women wallow in baths," he declared flatly.

"You seem to be a great authority on women and their habits," she said.

"You're damn right!" Adam replied morosely.

She didn't ask where he had acquired this vast knowledge, concluding that it must come from a series of tempestuous affairs. Even though *she* didn't like him, she had to admit most women would find him attractive. He wasn't her type, of course; she found him far too noisy. She preferred cautious, quiet men like Nigel, not ranters like Adam Deverell.

"You want me to draw a bath for her?" Lilly asked.

Daisy felt her cheeks growing hot. "What's the matter? Are you afraid I'll take more than my share of water?"

Perhaps this wasn't diplomatic under the circumstances, but she was getting heartily sick of people mistrusting her, and Lilly's suspicious attitude, coupled with Adam's visible disdain, didn't help her to behave tactfully.

She looked at Adam defiantly. "I will draw my own bath. You can check it before I get into it if you want to."

"Don't be silly." He grinned. "Come on, I'll show you which bathroom to use."

Cheeks still pink, she followed him up the broad staircase and along a corridor that showed signs of damage. He opened a double door and ushered her inside.

A double bed, dressing table and chest of drawers all covered in plastic sheeting were pushed against one wall, a trestle and a ladder beside them. Light filtered in through the plastic-covered windows and through the edges of the tarpaulin stretched across the roof.

"This is my Dad's bedroom. It was pretty well devastated," explain Adam, "but the bathroom's usable—if you don't mind not having a roof."

"I'm not looking for luxury," she said with a smile.

"Luxury's a commodity we're short of at the moment," he agreed.

"Being able to bathe is luxury enough," said Daisy, adding hastily, "even in two inches of water."

"You can have more than two inches." He gave her an unexpected smile and indicated a door leading off from the ruined bedroom. "Here you are. Lilly's already put out towels and soap."

Even in its battered state it was a lovely bathroom, spacious and airy with a tub that looked large enough to swim in. Lilly had left several peach-coloured towels on the edge of the tub, and soap, and even, Daisy noticed happily, a bottle of shampoo.

"I'm going to take a shower in the other wing," said Adam. "I'll meet you downstairs in half an hour."

In spite of the meagre amount of water she allowed herself it was the most enjoyable bath she'd ever had, and when she returned downstairs, her long strawberry-blond hair dripping down her back, she'd taken longer than the allotted half hour. But when she found Adam, closeted with a baldheaded man in a room containing a fax machine, computer terminal and several massive filing cabinets, he was too occupied to complain.

He looked up when she came in. "I'll be a while yet, Daisy," he said. It was the first time he had used her Christian name, and it sounded oddly right. As if he had known her for a long time.

The bald man smiled at her, and Adam said, "Daisy's a visitor here."

"Not a very good time to visit," said the man, and Daisy wondered if everyone prefaced introductions with this phrase. "I'm Trevor Stokes, Mr. Deverell's manager," he explained. "I won't keep Adam long."

He must have thought that she was a regular houseguest, or perhaps he thought she was Adam's lady, so she hastily said, "There's no hurry. I'll wait in the garden."

The garden would have been lovely before the storm. Now all the bushes were pruned and the trees stripped of leaves, but once it must have been ablaze with colour. And birds, she thought, there must have been lots of birds here, too. A tropical paradise.

She walked away from the house and found a pile of broken logs to sit on. Taking out her pad she made a rough sketch of the house. It would make a nice picture, even without the glory of a garden. She sketched in the men working on the roof. One of them wore a scarlet T-shirt that would make a nice contrast against the acid green of the buds.

Adam came out of the house wearing clean khaki shorts and a freshly ironed denim shirt. He had strong well-shaped legs, brown as nutmeg. He really had a very good body. He'd be a dream to paint in the nude, she thought idly. Imagining his expression if she suggested he strip off for her, she started to giggle.

He looked around, saw her sitting on her log and beckoned to her to join him. Cramming her pad back into her bag, she got up and ran across the grass to the Jeep. Her hair was dry now, and flew out behind her like a glossy silken banner. It felt so cool and fresh this way she couldn't bear to put the scarf back on. Surely, here there was no risk of discovery.

They were about to drive away when Lilly came out of the house and handed a basket up to him. "Sarah made some curry goat," she said. "You always liked curry goat."

Adam put the basket in the back of the Jeep. "Especially Sarah's. Thank her for me."

"She reckons she owes you. An' she does," she added when he protested. "An' I've put in a bit of my pineapple-spice cake. I still got plenty cornmeal."

"You won't have, if you keep making stuff for me," he said.

"I didn't jus' make it for you. We likes it, too," Lilly told him sternly.

He leaned down and kissed her cheek. "You make the best pineapple cake in Jamaica, Lilly."

"I know." She put a gnarled hand on his arm. "What am I supposed to tell Louise when she phones?" she demanded.

His brows drew into a frown. "Tell her to butt out of my life."

He drove away so quickly after that that Daisy was sure the old housekeeper didn't hear her when she thanked her for her hospitality. Not that Lilly's hospitality had been that great, come to think about it, but it never hurt to be polite.

It wasn't far from Solitaire Farm to the villa, but neither she nor Adam spoke. The mention of this character Louise seemed to have thrust him back into a black humour.

However, Daisy couldn't be bothered with him for she was suddenly overcome with fatigue. The combination of a relaxing bath and the sunlight gently caressing her through the trees had the same effect as a slug of Mogodon. It was only Adam's furious driving that kept her awake.

When they got back to Tamarind Cottage he stumped into the dining room, pulled a sheaf of papers from his briefcase and started working on them.

Fighting the temptation to go straight to bed, Daisy unpacked her suitcases. She found sheets in the bottom of the chest of drawers and made up the bed, and then she put the magazine with the "Marguerite, Where Are You?" article under her mattress. No point leaving that kind of evidence lying around.

It was now getting dark, and she decided to have a light meal and an early night.

She lit her stub of candle and went out to the kitchen. Adam was still working at the dining room table. As she passed him he stretched, yawning, the lamplight glinting on the dark hairs on his arms.

"That's enough for tonight," he muttered, pulling a bundle of magazines out of his briefcase. He started leafing through one. To her consternation she saw it was the same as the one she'd just hidden under her mattress. Her heart skipped a beat as he flicked idly through the pages, coming to rest at last in the business section.

She was safe for the moment, but sooner or later he'd come across that ghastly article, her secret would be out and he'd have the upper hand. She'd never be able to persuade him to let her stay.

CHAPTER FOUR

HER MIND WENT into overdrive.

As if suddenly overcome with the cold, she gave an exaggerated shiver and headed back to her bedroom. Once there she whipped her copy of the magazine from its hiding place, removed the staples from its spine and took out the entire arts section. She put the offending pages back under the mattress and carefully pressed the staples in the mutilated magazine flat again.

Hastily pulling her fisherman's jersey over her head, she pushed the magazine up under it and returned to the front room. Adam was now engrossed in an article in the travel section. In the kitchen she took a tin of soup from her case of supplies and put it on the draining board. Taking the tin opener from a hook on the wall, she returned to the dining room.

"I don't seem to be able to make this work," she said plaintively.

He stared at her over the top of his glasses. "What are you planning to open?"

"Some soup."

He went back to his magazine. "Lilly gave me enough curried goat for two. Save your soup for another day."

"I don't *want* curried goat," she shrilled. "I...I'm not very hungry. I just want a bowl of soup." She waggled the tin opener under his nose. *"Please!"*

He sighed. "Am I never to be free of persistent women?" But he took the opener from her and went into the kitchen.

Quick as a flash she whipped the magazine out from under her jersey and exchanged it for the one he had been reading.

"You're being very difficult," he said from the kitchen alcove. "We don't have refrigeration here, and Lilly always gives me too much food. Your tins will keep, the goat won't."

"I've never eaten goat," she said. "I'm not sure I'd like it."

"Nothing ventured nothing gained. Surely you're the adventurous type."

"Not particularly." She folded her arms in front of her and the magazine under her jersey crackled ominously.

"I can't believe that. A girl with no sense of adventure doesn't travel all this way to paint flowers. I'm asking you to share my dinner, Miss Gordon," he said tartly, "not share my life. Food's scarce here. It would be wise to accept."

"Well...all right," she said. Realizing that she sounded ungracious, she added, "It's just that I feel badly taking your food. When there are such shortages."

He put the unopened tin aside. "You don't have to. You can contribute something. What do you have in that Pandora's box of yours?"

Not wanting to join him in the kitchen in case the magazine rustled, or worse still slipped from beneath her jersey, she stayed where she was. "I have a packet of instant rice."

"Perfect. Rice is a great luxury these days."

"I'll cook it," she offered, "but first I...er...I have to put on some socks."

She darted into her room and shut the door. Safely concealed she thrust the magazine under the mattress, together with the torn pages. Tomorrow she'd burn them, or drop them down a ditch somewhere, anything as long as they were gone.

Adam had put the stew on to warm when she returned, thick white socks pulled over her ankles. She might have thought that all she wanted was a bowl of soup, but now that the aromatic smell of curry filled her nostrils she was overcome with hunger. It was all she could do not to cram a handful of raw rice into her mouth and chew on that.

She rummaged about in her case of food and found a packet of shortbread biscuits and ate one of those. "How about these for pudding?" she asked through a mouthful of crumbs. She held the box aloft.

Adam, who had returned to his magazine, glanced up briefly. "Great! This dinner is turning into a banquet."

"I don't think rice and biscuits are a banquet," she said.

"You will after a few weeks here," Adam replied laconically.

She measured water for the rice into a saucepan, and was looking around for the salt when Adam said, "That's peculiar." He was flicking through the magazine pages. "There's a section missing."

"Is there?" she said a trifle too brightly. "Do you like your rice al dente or well done?"

"Al dente. It looks as if I've already been done!'

She gave what she hoped sounded like a carefree chuckle, and babbled, "My! That curry smells good."

He turned the magazine over in his hands. "Somebody seems to have been mucking around with the staples. Things have come to a pretty pass when people start stealing the pages out of your reading matter."

Daisy made a strangled sound at the back of her throat.

"Well, to hell with it!" He tossed the magazine aside. "How about a rum before dinner?"

She was relieved that he'd dropped the subject, but she didn't think she should push her luck. Alcohol could make her careless, so she said, "I don't think I should take your drink as well as your food."

He got up from the chair in one athletic movement. "It's not my drink, it's Tilly's. I reckon he owes us both a drink."

"You do have a point." She smiled. It was the first time she'd smiled at him. He reached across her to get the bottle of rum from an upper cupboard. He was so close she could feel the warmth radiating from him, smell his clean male scent. Nigel had always smelt of carbolic soap and mouthwash. Adam smelt of sunshine, and pinewoods and good fresh earth.

"With water or orange juice?" he asked.

Because being so close to him unsettled her, she answered indecisively, "I don't know."

"Well, it had better be one or the other. Tilly drinks the local potion, and it's strong."

She settled for orange juice, then took her glass with her into the living room. There were two armchairs covered in faded striped cotton, facing an electric fire that was, of course, useless now. He sat in one, his long bare legs stretched out in front of him, ankles crossed, and she perched on the edge of the other. There were drops of water on the windows. It was raining again.

Because she was tired she was sensitive to the chill, and she shivered. "I must say your climate's a disappointment. This is just like home."

He regarded her thoughtfully. "And where's that?"

She was instantly wary and thought of lying. Of suggesting vaguely, "Somewhere in London," but since she didn't know the city she wasn't sure she could handle any questions he might ask. "I live in a small village," she mumbled, "in Cornwall. You wouldn't have heard of it."

"You never know. I might have."

"Is Jamaica always this wet?" she asked brightly.

"If you make the mistake of coming in the rainy season. Sensible visitors avoid October and November."

"Doesn't Mr. Tilson Brown come in November?"

He snorted into his glass. "What ever gave you the idea that Tilly was sensible?"

"Now that you mention it, he did seem a bit of a twit," she giggled. She could hear the wind lashing at the trees outside and she took a sip from her glass. She'd never cared for rum before, but this drink tasted good, and it warmed her. "Does it always blow so hard? I mean, apart from hurricanes."

"Not always. We're having an odd season this year."

"I gathered that." He was staring moodily into space, and she added, "I'm sorry about your coffee crop. I couldn't help overhearing. Is it very bad?"

"The maddening thing is," he said, "that at first it didn't seem to be. Oh, we lost a lot of berries during the storm, but we still had bearing trees. But then Trevor noticed that they're drying up, which means that the root system has been affected."

He looked suddenly so discouraged that she felt an inexplicable urge to reach out and comfort him. It must be the rum! she thought. She took a grip on herself. "Does it mean you'll have to sell up?"

He seemed to mentally shake himself. "Nothing that drastic. It means a massive replanting program, and a lot of work—and time—and I don't have much of that to spare. I want to get home."

"You mean to your beach house?" she asked.

He surprised her by saying, "I mean to England."

"You live in *England*!" she said, astounded. Although there was no reason why he shouldn't.

"And I don't intend to move," he replied with unnecessary vehemence.

"Nobody's asking you to." Honestly, she thought, she had no patience with him. She'd never met anyone so touchy.

"That's all you know," he muttered. Then he said, "That rice will be mush if we don't eat soon."

It wasn't mush, but it wasn't al dente, either. The curried goat, however, was so good the rice didn't seem to matter. She had two helpings, and several biscuits, and by the time they reached the coffee stage she was feeling warm as toast and drowsy.

The food seemed to have mellowed Adam as well, and when he said, "I didn't mean to bark at you earlier. I guess I'm edgier than I realized," she found it easy to smile at him.

"Forget it!"

"The one thing I'll miss in England is my constant supply of Blue Mountain coffee," he said ruefully. "I'm spoiled for anything else."

She took a sip of the dark fragrant brew. "I can see it could become addictive. I won't have the gall to offer you my instant after this."

He looked bleak. "I'm afraid instant's what we'll be reduced to very soon. We'll be lucky if we have enough to meet our Japanese commitment."

"You sell coffee to Japan?"

He nodded. A lock of hair fell untidily across his forehead. "The Japanese love Jamaican coffee."

"I'm not surprised." She gave a gigantic yawn and giggled. "And it doesn't seem to keep you awake, either."

"I suspect that's jet lag," he said. "I don't think we can use that as a sales pitch."

She yawned again, showing her even white teeth like a lovely tawny cat, and he said softly, "You really are a beautiful creature."

"I'm also very anti-men at the moment," said Daisy, sitting up sharply.

"No need to get twitchy. It so happens that I'm very anti-women, too, so you're quite safe."

"Well, you're not," she returned. "One false move and I'll brain you."

"I remember." He pretended to feel his head for the lump. "You swing a mean club."

"I could get meaner," she promised, "if I'm provoked."

"God forbid! I've had my share of irate females to date."

If she'd not been so weary she might have tried to find out just what he meant, but all she did was suggest they do the washing up before she fell asleep in her chair.

"Leave it!" he commanded. "The water truck should be here tomorrow. We can do them then. And Daisy..."

She stopped in the doorway of her bedroom. "You don't have to put that chair under the handle of your door. It wouldn't keep a flea out, and besides, I've never broken into a lady's bedroom in my life." He grinned cheerfully. "I always wait to be invited."

"You'll have to wait a long time then," she said, firmly shutting the door.

She slept fifteen hours straight. It was the water deliverymen yelling happily outside her window that woke her.

She lay still, listening to the clanking and the chatter, which was in such rich dialect that she couldn't understand a word. Contentedly she watched the fingers of sunlight streaming through the slats in the shutters. Then the truck chugged away and peace fell over the villa again.

She took her time getting washed and dressed. She peered dreamily out the window and watched a pair of hawks hovering below her in the cleft of the mountains, while she plaited her mane of hair into a ponytail and secured it with a leather thong.

In the kitchen Adam had put the dirty dishes into the sink, and she heated water and washed them and then had coffee and some cereal. She didn't intend to make a habit of doing Adam's washing up, but he had shared his dinner with her last night. It seemed a way of evening up the score.

She decided to spend the afternoon exploring on foot, and after putting her sketch pad into her day pack and slathering herself with protection cream, for her fair skin burned easily, she started climbing up the mountain.

It was a perfect day, the sky cloudless and the air crisp, the way it always was, even on the hottest day, in these high hills. Even the soggy, rain-soaked earth and the signs of Gilbert's rampage couldn't dull her pleasure. She turned off the road and climbed up to a small promontory. From here the sea glittered like crumpled foil in the distance, and she sat down on a rock and did a couple of rough drawings for her "sketch diary."

Her pencil moved with lightning strokes over the pad. The frustration that had been her constant companion ever since the publication of that first article about her and Paul Matheson started to fade. She had worried that she might have lost this ability to immerse herself in her work, but it was still with her, thank the Lord! Even the pain of her broken engagement was forgotten.

Jamaica hadn't been a mistake! It didn't matter that there were next to no flowers; it was still lovely here. Even a dozen hurricanes couldn't spoil the island's beauty. She had been overtired and jet-lagged yesterday when she thought she shouldn't have come. Her well-modelled lips curved in an unconscious smile, and she started to hum under her breath as she worked.

An hour later she returned her sketch pad to her pack and decided to follow a path that led upward toward the northern ridge. She had to climb over several felled trunks, and her running shoes slid on the muddy track, but the farther she walked the more entranced she became with the place. Particularly when she spied a splash of colour on one of the trees and found an orange orchid miraculously blooming on its trunk.

Hitching her pack more securely onto her back she clawed her way up to the plant. At close range the speckled delicacy of the flowers looked artificial against the bark. Wedging herself firmly in the branch she took out her sketchbook again and drew details of the fleshy blossoms, making notes about colour and texture, moving the leaves against the light to see the different effects.

She was so absorbed that when she heard a man's hoarse cry of fright she nearly fell off her branch. There was the sound of feet scrambling down the path, and Adam shouted, "Come back, man! It's not a duppy, it's a woman!"

"No human woman goin' to be hangin' on de trees...not in Nanny Town," another man cried.

Daisy peered over an overhanging rock at the top of Adam's khaki hat and said, "What *is* going on?"

"I thought it was you." He chuckled, "No duppy in these parts has strawberry-blond hair."

She started to slither down the incline. "And what exactly is a *duppy*?"

"A ghost. A spectre. A shade." She wobbled perilously at the edge of the path and he caught her in his arms. "My friend should have tried helping you down. He'd soon have discovered that you were solid enough."

Solid or not, he did not immediately let her go—and she did not try to break free. She didn't understand why, but she was glad to see him. Glad to be in the circle of his arms. For the length of a heartbeat they stood together.

Then, "What did your friend call this place?" she asked, stepping out of his embrace.

"Nanny Town."

"It sounds like a training school for mothers' helpers."

"Nothing so cosy," said Adam. "It's the name of a Maroon chief. Legend has it that no bullet ever harmed her."

"I'm really very ignorant, the only 'Maroon' I know is the colour."

"It was the name given to runaway slaves in the eighteenth century," said Adam. He took her arm, and it felt the most natural thing in the world to be arm in arm with him. "Were you on your way back to the villa?" he asked.

"I guess so," she said, falling into step beside him.

"Tell me more about these Maroons," she demanded, as much to fill the sudden tension between them as to glean information. "What did they do?"

"Fought for their freedom . . . for their lives. Some of them hid in Cockpit Country, some of them hid here, and they gave as good as they got. But in 1734 the English army dragged guns up the mountainside and their village was blown to bits. A few got away, but many threw themselves over the cliffs rather than surrender—"

"And now the place is haunted," Daisy finished for him. "Is that why your friend ran away?"

"Nanny Town is not a place most Jamaicans want to take a hike in," Adam said, smiling. "I'm not wild about it myself. They do say that if you camp overnight in this area white birds come and perch in tiers on the trees.''

''I wouldn't mind birds around me. I like birds.''

''You wouldn't like these,'' he promised. ''If you tried to shoot them your bullets would go right through them.'' Her feet skidded on some loose stones and he took her arm to steady her. His hand felt warm on her bare skin. ''What were you doing up in that tree anyway, apart from trying the scare the natives?''

''Making sketches of some orchids.'' She shot him a triumphant look from under her lashes. ''You see! There are still flowers in Jamaica. You just have to look for them, that's all.''

''You wouldn't have to look so hard in Falmouth,'' he reminded her.

She pulled her arm free. ''I happen to like the mountains.''

There was a slight chill between them after that, for she was annoyed with him for bringing up Falmouth again. She'd not yet thought up an unassailable reason for not going there, apart from the truth, and she didn't trust him enough to tell him that.

Back at the villa she busied herself fixing a meal for them from her supply of tins. ''It's my turn tonight,'' she insisted when he objected. ''It's only fair, after the curried goat.''

''Then Tilly will provide the wine,'' he said.

She looked doubtful. ''We seem to be drinking a lot of his liquor supply.'' But Adam waved such misgivings aside.

While Adam went to clean up, she opened a tin of tomato sauce and boiled water for spaghetti. He'd produced a tin of pears. Daisy marvelled at the irony of tinned fruit in the tropics and further rummaging unearthed a carton of grated mozzarella cheese that seemed edible.

Daisy wasn't a bad cook. She'd not had much opportunity to experiment since the only person she'd cooked for was Nigel and his tastes were limited. But she had imagination, and she enjoyed cooking. She poured a generous glassful of the red wine Adam had left out to "breathe" into the tomato sauce.

He came out of the bathroom. "Smells delicious," he said, leaning over her shoulder to sniff at the bubbling sauce.

"Mr. Heinz's best," she said, stirring it rather hard. Adam was wearing his navy towel again. Nothing else. Normally, naked, or nearly naked, men didn't disturb her; she'd painted enough nudes at art school not to throw a fit every time she saw a naked male. But there was something about this particular naked man that flustered her. She didn't understand it. After all, the towel covered more than a bathing suit would have done. But she seemed unable to concentrate on anything but the texture of his skin, the damp hair that curled on his chest and ran into a V on his hard muscled stomach.

"Excuse me," she said, "I'm just going to put on a jersey—I'm cold."

In her room she yanked her fisherman's knit over her head, and then freed her hair from its braided ponytail. "Idiot! *Idiot!*" she muttered to herself as she tugged the brush through a tangle. "It's *pathetic*! Panting over a half-naked man like a slobbering nympho." She put down the brush and looked at herself in the mirror. "Pull yourself together!" she ordered sternly.

She wasn't in the habit of talking to herself, but the situation seemed to call for it. Perhaps she was suffering from a form of sexual starvation, a condition triggered by the pain of her breakup with Nigel. Not that her relationship with Nigel had been particularly sexy, but clearly the loss of her man must have unleashed some deep-seated reaction in her psyche. Well, it simply wouldn't do. She must get a grip on herself at once. She took a deep breath and, setting her lips, went back to dish up the spaghetti.

But in spite of her resolve to keep Adam at a distance, the dinner became an intimate, cosy affair. Perhaps it was Mr. Tilson Brown's wine that made her feel so at ease, that made her giggle at Adam's stories and notice what attractive eyes he had when he was smiling. Made her aware of his strong brown fingers when he twirled spaghetti around his fork, and made her wonder how it would feel to have those fingers stroke her hair...her face....

Whatever it was, it lulled her into a state of false security, and when Adam started asking her questions about herself as they sat over their coffee, she answered without her usual caution.

"My father decided he'd had enough of responsibility, and left us when I was ten," she told him, "and then, when I was fifteen, my mother died."

"That's a rough age to lose your mother," he said softly.

She lifted slim shoulders under her heavy knit jersey. "It is. But I was lucky. The people my mother had been working for took me in. I think it had something to do with my love for art. The man was, ah, is an artist, and he'd always thought I had talent. They made it possible for me to go to art school." Her face clouded when she remembered the Mathesons' recent betrayal, and she said quietly, "I'll always be grateful for that at least."

"Is it because of your father that you're off the male sex?" he asked, and she looked at him blankly. "Didn't you tell me that you were anti-men? I wondered if it had something to do with your father."

"Oh! I got over that years ago. No, it's nothing to do with him, it's because of—" caution suddenly returned "—because of an . . . an unfortunate relationship."

Adam took a sip of coffee. "Were you involved with a married man?" he asked.

Her heart gave a sickening lurch. Did he know about the scandal? Because, of course, Paul was married to Peggy, who had caused all the trouble. "Of course not. No!"

"It's not unknown, angel."

"No . . . but it's nothing like that—" She could feel herself blushing.

"I didn't mean to upset you, Daisy," Adam said.

"You haven't. I mean..." She took a gulp of air. "I was engaged to be married, and...it fell apart. I suppose I'm still, er, in shock." She looked down at her hands, which were clasped tightly in her lap. "We'd been going together for three years," she added, hoping three years would give validity to this half-truth.

"How old are you, Daisy?"

"Twenty-three."

"Well, I'm ten years older, and believe me, you'll recover."

"You speak from experience, do you?" she said with some asperity. There was a smugness in his tone that annoyed her. He made thirty-three sound like Methuselah.

"Me! Good God, no! You wouldn't catch me getting myself entangled in an engagement. Engagements usually lead to marriage, and that's one path I have no intention of treading."

"Fine."

"Ever."

"Fine." She didn't know why his attitude annoyed her so much, but it did. It must be because he'd managed to shatter the lovely mood that had developed between them.

With a clatter of china she collected their coffee cups, and was distant with him for the rest of the evening.

CHAPTER FIVE

SHE SLEPT ANOTHER twelve hours that night, and when she woke the following morning to find the world swirling with mist and damp as a bath sponge, she felt better than she had in weeks.

She stayed indoors, working on her sketches, deciding which ones to keep and which to abandon. After a quick lunch of a couple of shortbread biscuits and a cup of instant coffee, which tasted quite dreadful after Adam's Blue Mountain, she went for a walk in the dripping world outside.

Today she stayed on the road, which was already running with water and in places seemed like a mountain stream. Overhead the clouds seemed to be resting on the treetops, like nets hung over giant fruit trees. From time to time she heard the melodious cooing of some ring-tailed pigeons, but apart from these sad-sounding birds all was muffled silence.

A sort of magic seemed to steal into her soul, as if the mountains were making her their own. Claiming her, so that no matter where she might go in the future part of her would always be here, among the *duppy*-haunted ceiba trees.

It was a friendly possession, and she didn't fight it. And when she had returned to the villa and made herself a cup of tea, she started work on a picture that she hoped would capture this sorcery of mist and trees and mountains.

She worked swiftly, overlapping the pale washes so that they would merge and blend into the "feeling" of the picture. By the time she had to light the lamp, the floor was strewn with discarded attempts. She had created one that didn't displease her too much. At least, one that she could use as inspiration for a better one.

She didn't look at her watch until Adam came in, bearing two avocados and a small pineapple. They had agreed last night that it made more sense to share their food and the kitchen chores, and tonight was his turn to provide dinner.

"Fresh fruit! I'll have to go into Kingston for some tomorrow," she exclaimed.

"These are gifts from friends. Fruit's still scarce in the shops, *and* it's expensive." He came over and squinted down at the watercolour. "That's *good*," he said. "That's very good indeed."

She laughed. "You don't need to sound so surprised." But she was pleased. She knew he was not a man who gave compliments easily.

"This sort of picture must give you more satisfaction than limiting yourself to flowers, doesn't it?" he asked.

"It depends." She washed out her brush and squeezed it dry between her fingers. "If I'm doing illustrations for a book on botany, painting flowers is very satisfying. Greetings cards are something else."

"Just the same—" he leaned over her, examining the picture more closely "—you should concentrate on this kind of abstract work. Get enough pieces together and have a show. This is evocative stuff."

She was very aware of his closeness, of the warmth that emanated from him. "Greeting cards are my bread and butter," she explained. "I can't afford to go abstract on a whim."

She had thought of it, though, of painting something more personally rewarding than bunches of pretty flowers to go with syrupy verses. But she had to earn her living, and besides, neither Paul nor Peggy had ever encouraged such a venture. "It's important to know one's limitations, sweetie," Peggy had often instructed her. "You have a nice little talent and you should be able to make a decent living, as long as you don't try flying too high."

And as Paul, who'd always encouraged Daisy, had offered no opinion, Daisy had taken Peggy's advice.

After dinner Adam went off somewhere in his Jeep, and she was left to amuse herself. And why not, she thought, he doesn't have to stay here and keep me company. But she wouldn't have believed that the villa would seem so empty without him.

Since they now had plenty of it, she heated water and had a wash in the bathtub. She shampooed her hair again, too. Then, wrapping herself in a kimono she'd picked up at a church sale, she padded into the kitchen to make a hot drink.

She heard the Jeep drive up, and bumping noises on the steps, then Adam called from the door. "Give me a hand, angel, will you?"

She put down the packet of powdered milk and went to the door. He had hauled a large desk up the steps and was attempting to manoeuvre it into the house.

"Find that in the forest, did you?" she teased.

"Give me a hand before I get a hernia," he said, grinning at her. "This is solid oak, I'll have you know."

When they had pulled the thing inside and Adam had fetched the drawers from the Jeep, Daisy asked, "Why are you doing this in the dead of night? Did you nick this little number?"

"You might put it that way." He started fitting the drawers back into the desk. "It comes from Solitaire. Lilly made quite a fuss, I can tell you."

"But *why*, Adam? There's enough furniture in this place, isn't there?"

"It's for you." He ran his hand over the highly polished wood. "For your painting."

"But I can use the dining room table," she protested, slightly daunted by the thought of Lilly's indignation.

"I need that," he said firmly. "I have to work, too, you know. Look—" he opened a drawer "—you can store your painting stuff in here!"

"Well, if you're sure...?"

"I am. Now where's the best light for you, angel?"

"Let's face it, there's only one lamp that's really bright, but you'll need that too," she said.

"I know!" he exclaimed, "we'll go coed. Very democratic." He proceeded to pull the desk next to the dining room table. "This way we can share the lamp, inspire each other and feel cosy at the same time."

He grinned with satisfaction, then he leaned forward, took her face in his hands and kissed her very lightly on the tip of her nose. "I've always thought, though, that kissing is about the cosiest thing you can do," he said softly before releasing her.

It had been the most innocent of kisses, brief, and light as a butterfly's wing, but its effect on Daisy was astonishing. She felt as if her legs might give way beneath her. "Are...are you sure they won't miss the desk at Solitaire?" she croaked anxiously, playing for time.

"Who could miss it? Dad's in Australia, and neither Lilly nor Sarah use it." His eyes danced with laughter. "I do believe you're shaking, angel. Afraid Lilly might come tearing up here in the dead of night to claim it?"

He knew why she was shaking. Of course he did, and Daisy cursed herself for being so transparent. For wanting him so much. "As a matter of fact I'm cold," she said, moving away. "My hair's still wet."

"Angel!" He was all contrition. "Did I get you out of the bath?"

"No. No, I was finished, but I was feeling chilly. I was just going to have a cup of cocoa while my hair dried."

He guided her firmly toward one of the armchairs. "I'll dry your hair for you. Where's the towel?"

"It's nearly dry now. Really," she objected weakly. She had hoped that mentioning something as prosaic as wet hair and cocoa might neutralize the charged atmosphere, but the reverse seemed to be happening.

Adam returned from the bathroom with a towel. "I'm very good at this," he informed her, leaning over the chair back and towelling vigorously. "I've had a lot of experience."

The silk of her robe was so thin she could almost believe he would see her heart thumping in her breast. "Oh? Did you once work in a hair salon then?" she said with false brightness.

"No, angel. I've just had a lot of women in my life."

"I don't think it's very gallant to boast about it." The feel of his strong hands rubbing her scalp was making every nerve in her body tingle.

"Who's boasting? By and large it hasn't been particularly pleasant, as a matter of fact."

His hands were moving more slowly now, rhythmically round and round her scalp until she thought she would jump out of her skin with longing. She tried slumping slightly in her chair in an effort to escape this delicious pressure, although escape was really the last thing she wanted. "Perhaps you should give them up," she quavered.

"Give what up, angel?" he asked, his lips against her ear.

"Wo...women." She reached under the towel. "I...I think I'm dry."

"I wouldn't want to give up *all* women. Just the annoying ones." He unwound the towel and buried his face in her hair. "You smell wonderful." His voice was husky. "Like summer flowers."

"Th...that's the shampoo." She was amazed that words could still come out of her throat, it felt so tight.

"It has nothing to do with the shampoo, angel," he said with a soft laugh. "You're so delicate and fine.... You remind me of a flower yourself."

"Appearances can be deceptive," said Daisy, swallowing hard. "Actually I'm as tough as old boots."

He looked suddenly serious. "No, angel," he said, "I don't think you are."

"I'm never ill."

"I wasn't talking about your health. There's another kind of toughness. You don't have it, thank goodness."

"Maybe I should acquire a tougher hide. At least it would keep the chill out." She tried to appear decisive. "Time for that hot drink, I think. Do you want a cup of cocoa, too?"

"No, angel, I don't want cocoa." He smoothed back a strand of her hair, and she noticed that his hand was trembling. Then, very deliberately, he took off his glasses, tilted her head back and kissed her firmly on the mouth.

It was as if she'd waited all her life for this moment. Her lips opened softly under his.

When the kiss ended he came around to the front of her chair. He pulled her gently to her feet and held her close. "Darling Daisy," he murmured into her drift of silky hair, "kissing you is like kissing fresh snow. You're flawless."

She gave a little fluttering sigh and laid her head on his shoulder. He started to caress her, running his hands rhythmically up and down her back, feeling the delicacy of her spine through the thin silk of her kimono.

A voluptuous mixture of languor and excitement began to build in Daisy's slender body and when he kissed her again, with an urgency that made her pulses leap, she responded with answering passion.

At last he took his lips from hers and, pulling the kimono aside, kissed her shoulders and the base of her white throat where her pulse was beating wildly.

"You're so beautiful," he murmured, "the most beautiful thing...."

She wound her arms round his neck, drawing him closer. "Adam...Oh, Adam!"

"Oh, Daisy!" he murmured hoarsely. "You're so clean...so unspoiled."

"Kiss me!" she cried, all caution flown. "Kiss me, Adam!"

"Angel!" He brought his lips down on hers and held her tight. She could feel the play of his hard muscles against her body, feel the heat of him.

His hand found and stroked her breast. "I want you, sweetheart. I've wanted you since the moment I first saw you," he whispered.

"Not quite the first moment," she reminded him between kisses.

"Don't quibble, darling," he said, his breath ragged. "I want you now. I want to make love to you until you faint with pleasure."

"Yes, oh, yes!" she gasped, and the kimono slipped off her body and slid into a pool of indigo silk on the floor.

She stood before him, glowing and beautiful. Waiting for him to gather her in his arms and carry her into his bedroom. To love her until the world was a spinning diamond in the velvet night ...

But he didn't gather her into his arms. Instead he reached down, picked up the kimono and draped it over her white shoulders. "You're very lovely, Daisy," he said gruffly. "And very giving. But ... but I think perhaps I'd better have that cup of cocoa after all."

If he had hit her face, slapped her again and again, she couldn't have felt more brutalized. She clutched the thin silk tightly around her body, crossing her arms over her breasts protectively.

"Help yourself," she said through stiff lips. "I'm going to bed." She turned scarlet and added, "On my own."

She took two steps toward the safety of her bedroom, but he caught her arm and turned her to face him. "Angel, please understand...."

The color flooded again into Daisy's delicate face. "You don't have to apologize just because you had second thoughts," she said bitterly.

"It's not that I don't *want* to make love to you, Daisy. You're the most beautiful creature I've ever seen...." A vein throbbed at his temple.

"You needn't try to explain, Adam." She pulled her arm free and went on in a remarkably even voice, "Believe me, I do understand."

She didn't really. The only thing she knew was that he'd rejected her. Humiliated her cruelly, and now all she wanted was to get away from him. Because now, she hated him. Hated him for his thoughtless brutality.

"Darling—" he said.

She cut in quickly. "Don't call me that!"

He put his hands on her shoulders again, and she flinched away from him as if she'd been burned. "Daisy, please. The last thing I meant to do was hurt you...."

"I'm not hurt," she lied. "Making love was probably a bad idea. I think you did us both a favor with your—" she pulled her mouth into a cynical smile "—your *admirable* self-control."

"Oh, hell!" he exploded. "Stop *talking* like that. It's not your style, angel."

"And what exactly *is* my style?" she asked with overloaded politeness.

"Simplicity."

"You mean simpleminded, don't you?" she said, as close to a sneer as she'd ever come in her life.

"No, dammit! I don't. I mean simple. *Trusting.* And I don't want to be the one to betray that trust, Daisy."

"How serious you are," she said, and because the hurt he'd inflicted still burned like acid, she added,

"I've never met a man who made such a fuss about a little roll in the hay."

He regarded her thoughtfully for a second. "Haven't you?" he said quietly. "Well, I'm a funny chap."

"Hilarious!" She tightened the sash of her kimono. "And now, I'm going to bed. Good night!"

Lying as stiff as a board on her mattress, Daisy listened to Adam moving around in the other room, heard his muffled curse when he dropped a glass. She would never forgive him. Never. A decent man wouldn't treat even a...a casual pickup the way he'd treated her. Urging her to heights of passion she hadn't known she possessed, only to turn away at the very moment of surrender. Shame still swept over her with every pulse of her blood.

Daisy was not an experienced girl. She'd lived all her life in a small community, and during her years at art school she'd been too busy with her studies to have much time for men. There had been boyfriends, of course, but nothing more than that. And then Nigel had come into her life. Nigel hadn't been particularly passionate, and Daisy had assumed that she must have a low sex drive herself, for his lack of interest had not bothered her. But the ardent, glowing woman who had stood before Adam was not a woman with a low sex drive. She was certainly not a woman Nigel would have recognized...or have wanted to know, in all probability.

Perhaps that had been the problem with Adam. Perhaps she'd been too fervent in her response? Recalling her urgent "Yes, oh, yes!" A new wave of shame swept over her.

She fell asleep eventually, but it was fitful slumber, broken with anxious dreams.

SHE WOKE TO SUNLIGHT slanting across the shutters, latticing the floor with stripes of light. "Coffee. Or do you want tea?" asked Adam from the door. He was dressed in shorts and T-shirt.

She sat up in the rumpled bed, holding the sheet tight against her breasts. "I want you to stay out of my bedroom," she snapped.

He looked at her somberly. "About last night," he said. "I took advantage of you...."

Always scrupulously honest in her dealings with people, Daisy said, "I don't remember fighting you off."

"You're a very beautiful woman, angel. The most desirable women I've ever met. But right now—" he gave an impatient sigh "—right now the timing's all wrong."

She glared at him with open hostility. "I really don't want to discuss it, Adam." He pushed his glasses farther up his nose. *Hiding behind them,* she thought. *Coward!*

He said, "The decent thing to do would be to move out and leave the villa to you—"

"Which is what I've been asking you to do since you arrived," she reminded him.

"—because if we share the same roof I don't think I can stop myself from trying to make love to you again."

He might be saying that simply to pour oil on troubled waters, although from the little she did know of him she doubted it. Tact didn't appear to be his strong suit.

"Don't worry, I won't give you a second chance," she assured him grimly. "But under the circumstances surely the best thing would be for you to move out."

He shook his head. "No way, Daisy. You wouldn't be safe here. Not on your own."

"I find that hard to believe."

He set his jaw stubbornly. "I don't care whether you do or not, it happens to be a fact. So I stay on, and stay out of your way as much as I can." He smiled wryly for the first time that morning. "And I promise I'll do my best to behave like a gentleman."

"That'll make a nice change," she murmured sourly. "And now if you don't mind, I'd like to get dressed."

"There's coffee in the kitchen," he said. "I'm off now, I've got work to do."

When he'd gone she dressed in her favourite pink jeans, and plaited her hair in two thick braids. She felt a little better, and paradoxically was pleased because he was staying on in the villa. But she still felt slightly sick to her stomach when she remembered her impassioned surrender.

She saw Adam rarely during the next two weeks. He stayed out of her way, only coming home late in the evening to share a meal.

She usually worked at her desk for a couple of hours after dinner, and sometimes he went through official-looking papers or blueprints at the table, but mostly he went straight to bed, which was understandable since he was up and out of Tamarind Cottage before dawn.

Gradually they recovered some of their old rapport, and her sense of humiliation began to fade. There was still a tingle of sexual tension between them, but they both scrupulously ignored it. And they never, never touched. Not even in the most innocent way.

Daisy spent a lot of this time driving around in her rented car, searching for the few flowering bushes left standing. When she was lucky she watched scissor-tailed hummingbirds sip nectar from the deep throats of scarlet flowers, and caught glimpses of orange-and-black orioles darting through the trees. The weather had turned warm and turkey buzzards drifted in a sky that glittered like opal. Hawks swooped and hovered in the sunshine, and lizards sunned themselves lethargically on smooth tree trunks.

She visited crowded markets that were woefully short on produce, but rich in exotic characters. She filled sketchbook after sketchbook, and each night painted her impression of all she'd seen until her eyes gave out.

She usually drove home by way of Devil's Gully. Although the road was spectacularly bad, the view was breathtaking. Sometimes she would see Adam's Jeep parked among the tangle of shanties, and catch a glimpse of his naked back as he worked alongside his men. Not that this had anything to do with her choice of route, she told herself sternly. She simply enjoyed the scenery.

Once she went to Solitaire to collect their laundry. The roof was on now, and the house restored to its former elegance, but it was not a pleasant visit. Lilly met her at the door, and glared at her with such venom that Daisy felt quite uncomfortable. She tried to make polite conversation but the old woman remained monosyllabic and she got out of there as quickly as she could.

One day she got back to the villa earlier than usual. She'd taken a trip to the beautiful old town of Port Antonio, where she'd bought a fresh fish for their dinner, after learning Port Antonio was famous for its deep-sea fishing.

The sun was starting to slip down toward the sea, and she was looking forward to a quiet cup of tea while she browsed through the day's batch of sketches.

She turned into the driveway to find it blocked by an immaculate-looking estate car. She backed down the drive again and, leaving her car on the road, approached the house on foot.

She'd heard enough stories about looting to feel slightly nervous, but she didn't think even the most sanguine of thieves would park quite so obviously. Besides the car looked too comfortable to be owned by thieves.

She was just mounting the front steps when the door flew open and a small, dark-haired woman shot out. "Yes?" the woman said belligerently. "What can I do for you?"

Daisy coolly held her ground. "I happen to be living here," she said. "And you're trespassing."

The strange woman took a step forward, hissing like an enraged goose. "So you're the one, are you?" she cried. "You're the slut who's shacking up with Adam."

CHAPTER SIX

DAISY WAS TOO ASTOUNDED to do more than say, "He was here when I moved in," which, on reflection, didn't quite set the right tone.

"I could kill him," the little woman spat venomously, "fooling around with you when he said he was working. Never returning my phone calls—"

That triggered a memory. "Why, you must be Louise!" Daisy cried.

"Oh! he told you about me, did he?" She gave Daisy a hostile look. Then she looked again and said, "Do I know you?"

"No," said Daisy hastily. Recognition on top of everything else was more than she could cope with. "But Lilly's mentioned you."

"She's mentioned you, too," the woman said bitterly. "Told me how Adam brought you to Solitaire...gave you a bath..." She glared accusingly.

"I think Lilly's been exaggerating," Daisy said.

"Do you?" The woman sneered. "Well, let me tell you that if it wasn't for Lilly I wouldn't know *what* Adam was up to."

A nasty suspicion was beginning to form in Daisy's mind. She was about to suggest that it might be more useful to stop snarling at each other and have a calm talk over a cup of tea, when a small girl came to the open doorway.

"Can I have one of these, Mummy?" she asked. She was clutching an unopened packet of digestive biscuits, part of Daisy's food supply.

"Put that back where you found it, Cathy," her mother commanded. "It doesn't belong to you."

"But I'm so hungry my stomach's touching my backbone," the child wailed.

"You're not hungry, you're *gravalishus*!" her mother snapped, falling into dialect in her irritation.

The child stuck out a familiarly obstinate chin. "Hunger is not the same as greed, an' I'm *hungry*." And then she looked at Daisy and gave her an impish grin. She was the spitting image of Adam, from her dark wayward curls to the glasses perched on her freckled nose.

It was all the proof Daisy needed. The horrible suspicion that had been growing was confirmed. Adam was married. He was married and this little girl was obviously his daughter.

No wonder his wife—for Louise must be his wife—was furious. He must have deserted her, left her without letting her know where he'd gone. He'd done a bunk, fled the marital coop like the rat he was, and was now shirking his responsibilities here in the mountains. That was why he didn't return his wife's phone calls, and—Daisy felt the heat rise in her body—it was why he was toying with the idea of an illicit affair with his unexpected visitor into the bargain.

"Don't go away!" she said to the angry little woman. "I'm going to get Adam. He's got some explaining to do."

"I'm not going anywhere," Louise promised, adding sarcastically, "it's nice that *one* of us knows where to find him."

It so happened that Daisy had returned through Devil's Gully that afternoon and had seen Adam's Jeep parked there. She only hoped he hadn't left. Not that it mattered. Somebody would know where he was and she'd rout him out if she had to go to hell itself, for she was consumed with a mounting, righteous rage.

As she drove into the mountains at a speed that even by Jamaican standards would have been considered unsafe, she recounted those enigmatic remarks he had dropped from time to time.

What was it he'd said when he'd so expertly towelled her hair dry? "I've just had a lot of women in my life." He must have been referring to his wife and child. Anti-women indeed! Anti-marriage was more like it.

She stabbed down hard on the accelerator and nearly drove off the side of the road. No wonder Lilly had been so hostile. Remembering the unfriendly reception she'd been given when she went for their laundry, Daisy felt her blood pressure rise another notch. What a louse he was, putting her in that position. He must have known how Lilly would react.

As she drove she grew angrier and angrier, but her rage was not just directed at Adam. It was directed at *all* the men who'd let her down in her life, starting with her father, whom she'd loved and who had walked away from her without so much as a goodbye when she was ten. And meek Paul Matheson, so helpful when Daisy was trying to cope after her mother's death, but quite willing to cash in on a lie. And what about Nigel? Safe, self-satisfied Nigel. The man she had chosen to share her life with. No matter how much she protested her innocence, he had refused to believe her; but he seemed more than ready to play the forgiving martyr if it made him look good in the papers.

And Adam was the biggest rat of the bunch. He was a lying, evasive hypocrite! If there was one failing Daisy despised above all others it was hypocrisy. Why couldn't he have been honest with her and told her from the start that he was a married man?

But of course he wouldn't have done that. He would have expected that she would send him packing immediately. No matter how attracted she might have been to him, there was no way she would have allowed him to stay on. Ironically, it now seemed fortunate that he'd suffered that last-minute attack of conscience, or whatever it was that had stopped him from taking her when she had so rashly offered herself. She supposed she should feel grateful about that, even if it was only the dread of a clinging mistress that had stopped him.

She hurtled into Devil's Gully, scattering chickens before her, and drew up with a squeal of tires when she saw the Jeep parked on the edge of the road. A little way up the hill she spied Adam, stripped to the waist, surveying the frame of a new house. Trevor Stokes was with him.

The sight of his brown back added fuel to her fury. She remembered too well the feel of his flesh under her hands. Giving an angry sob, she grabbed the fish she'd bought for their supper, and started running up the hill.

Trevor must have seen her first, for he said something and Adam turned, smiling warmly. "Daisy! How nice," he said, when she came to a halt before him.

Holding the fish firmly by its tail, she swung it around her head. "You rat!" she screamed. "You snake in the grass!" The fish, divested of its wrapping paper, caught Adam squarely in the face. "You are the biggest liar—"

She went to whirl her fishy club again, but he caught her wrist. "What's the matter with you?" he demanded. "Have you taken leave of your senses?"

"No, I've come to them, you double-crosser," she panted, wriggling.

He took a firmer grip on her wrist. "Stop trying to hit me with that stinking fish."

"I wish it was a . . . a baseball bat!" she choked. "Something that makes a lasting impression." He shook her wrist and the fish dropped to the ground. "The scales," she declared breathlessly, "have fallen from my eyes."

"They certainly have. They're all over my glasses." He took off his glasses and started wiping them with his handkerchief. "What was it? Red snapper?"

Her lip curled. "Don't try being winsome, Adam. It won't wash."

"No one's ever accused me of that," said Adam.

Trevor suppressed a grin. "I guess I'm in the way here," he said.

When Trevor was out of earshot, Adam said, "Now will you please get a grip on yourself and explain what this is all about."

"I've found out the truth," announced Daisy, her magnificent tawny eyes emitting sparks, "that's what!"

"*What* truth, for God's sake?" He put his glasses back on and glared at her through the smeary lenses. "You come roaring into Devil's Gully waving seafood around like a demented mermaid—"

"Someone is waiting to see you back at the villa," informed Daisy.

"So what?"

"Your *wife* is waiting," she declared dramatically.

Adam raised his eyebrows. "You," he said, "have had too much sun."

"It's no good, Adam." She was suddenly sick of verbal fencing. "I've talked to Louise. She's there with your daughter—"

"My daughter?"

"Don't try and deny it. Her name is Cathy and she's the image of you."

"So are Amanda and Sue. It drives their father wild." He raised an inquiring eyebrow. "Did Louise *tell* you we were married?"

"Well…" she faltered, "ah, not in so many words."

"I'm glad to hear it. My sister has been known to stretch the truth, but I didn't think she'd go that far."

"Louise is your *sister*?" A stone seemed to roll off her heart.

"One of them. I'd better go and see what she wants, I suppose." He reached over to where his shirt was hanging on a tree stump and started to pull it on. "You're not going to hit me again, are you?" he asked, when she bent down to retrieve the fish.

"Supper!" she explained, brushing dirt off the fish's rosy back. "No point wasting it." She looked up at him, her eyes dark golden in the late-afternoon light. "Oh, Adam! I do feel such a fool."

He leaned forward and tugged one of her shiny plaits. "So you should. Frightening poor Trevor out of his wits like that."

"Poor Trevor thought it highly entertaining." She gave a rueful grin. "I *am* sorry, Adam."

"Forget it. Now give me half an hour to hear what Louise has to say, and then perhaps we can spend the rest of the evening in peace." When they got to his Jeep, he asked, "Was Louise rude to you?"

"She didn't exactly sing 'Welcome to Jamaica.'" The setting sun was at her back, turning her hair to flame. "She seemed to think we were living in sin."

"None of her damn business," growled Adam.

"Maybe not," she agreed, "but just the same..."

He put his fingers under her chin. "Forget Louise," he said. "The important thing is—are we friends again?"

She smiled lightly, although at his touch her heart had started banging away like a drum. "If you want."

Brushing her lips lightly with his own, he murmured, "I want."

It was as if the late-afternoon sunlight that burnished the treetops had entered her soul. *He's free . . . he's free . . .* sang her heart.

Then why did he reject you that night? asked her head soberly. She decided to ignore both of them.

"See you later, then," she said with an airy wave. She'd take a look at the village and give Adam time to deal with his sister.

It seemed very quiet in Devil's Gully after he'd driven off. Far below cattle grazed, some of the cows with snow-white cattle egrets on their backs. To her left the mountains fell away in a series of sharp-topped hills, vivid with fresh green foliage. Several shacks clung tenaciously to them. She could make out the shadowy figure of a woman sitting on one of the rickety porches. Daisy raised her hand in greeting and soon the woman, accompanied by two small barefoot girls, came down to investigate the stranger.

She was quickly joined by several more adults and a scattering of children, all of whom started to question Daisy rapidly in an accent so thick she had difficulty understanding. But judging from their smiles they were friendly, and soon her ear became more accustomed to the sound of their singsong dialect.

"Is you a tourist?" one old man asked.

A little boy answered scornfully, "She no tourist, man. She got no camera." He looked crestfallen. "I sure was hopin' you'd have a camera, missus," he told Daisy. "I wanted to get my picture took."

"I'll *draw* your picture if you like," Daisy offered, taking her sketch pad from her purse.

There were several delighted oohs and aahs as the group crowded round, watching her pencil catch the child's likeness in a few deft strokes. She tore off the page and handed it to the boy when she'd finished.

"That's real *crisp*!" he said, showing it to his friends.

Offering to draw his picture had seemed like a good idea at the time, but now *everyone* wanted his or her picture drawn, and it was only when Daisy pointed out that it was too dark to see properly that they agreed to let her go.

"I'll come back tomorrow and draw the rest of you," she promised.

The purple shadows lay thick in the mountains when she set off for the villa. She was looking forward to seeing Adam, to telling him of her little adventure. As she drove, she found herself again engaged in the little war between her head and her heart.

He declined to make love to you before, her head reminded her. *Don't be a fool. Don't put yourself in that humiliating position again.*

But her heart bubbled, *Shut up, killjoy! He's waiting for me now. Later on . . . who knows what might happen?*

Adam wasn't the only one waiting at the villa, however. The station wagon was still parked in the drive. Cursing mildly under her breath, Daisy left her car on the road again.

"I was beginning to wonder if you were all right," said Adam, when she went in. He and Louise were sitting in the armchairs, a tray with dirty teacups on the table between them. The child, Cathy, was perched on Adam's knee, playing with a doll.

Daisy went into the kitchen area and carefully put the fish onto a plate. "I hung around sketching the residents," she said.

Louise stood. Now that Daisy knew who she was she could see that she resembled her brother, though not to the same startling degree as Cathy. "We must go," said Louise. "George will be screaming for his supper."

"George never screams," said Adam. He nodded toward the kitchen. "Daisy's back. You can say your piece now."

Louise's lips tightened imperceptibly. "Adam tells me I made a mistake, that I jumped to conclusions..." She trailed off.

Daisy cut in with a smile. "Forget it! It was perfectly natural."

Louise didn't smile back. "You must admit the situation does rather ask for gossip. If you want my opinion—"

"We don't," Adam said. His sister scowled at him.

Not wanting to be party to a family squabble, Daisy said firmly. "As far as I'm concerned Adam can move out any time he wants."

WOW!

THE MOST GENEROUS
FREE OFFER EVER!

From the Harlequin Reader Service®

GET 4 FREE BOOKS WORTH $10.00

Affix peel-off stickers to reply card

PLUS A FREE VICTORIAN PICTURE FRAME

AND A FREE MYSTERY GIFT!

NO COST! NO OBLIGATION TO BUY!
NO PURCHASE NECESSARY!

Because you're a reader of Harlequin romances, the publishers would like you to accept four brand-new Harlequin Romance® novels, with their compliments. Accepting this offer places you under no obligation to purchase any books, ever!

ACCEPT FOUR BRAND-NEW

YOURS

We'd like to send you four free Harlequin novels, worth $10.00, to introduce you to the benefits of the Harlequin Reader Service®. We hope your free books will convince you to subscribe, but that's up to you. Accepting them places you under no obligation to buy anything, but we hope you'll want to continue your membership in the Reader Service.

So unless we hear from you, once a month we'll send you 6 additional Harlequin Romance® novels to read and enjoy. If you choose to keep them, you'll pay just $2.24* per volume—a saving of 26¢ off the cover price, plus only 69¢ shipping and handling for the entire shipment! There are no hidden extras! And you may cancel at anytime, for any reason, just by sending us a note or a shipping statement marked "cancel." You can even return any shipment to us at our expense. Either way, the free books and gifts are yours to keep!

ALSO FREE!
VICTORIAN PICTURE FRAME

This lovely Victorian pewter-finish miniature is perfect for displaying a treasured photograph—and it's yours *absolutely free*—when you accept our no-risk offer.

Perfect for a treasured Photograph

Plus a FREE mystery Gift! follow instructions at right.

*Terms and prices subject to change without notice. © 1990 Harlequin Enterprises Limited

HARLEQUIN ROMANCE® NOVELS

FREE!

 Harlequin Reader Service®

```
AFFIX
FOUR FREE BOOKS
STICKER HERE
```

YES, send me my four free books and gifts as explained on the opposite page. I have affixed my "free books" sticker above and my two "free gift" stickers below. I understand that accepting these books and gifts places me under no obligation ever to buy any books; I may cancel at anytime, for any reason, and the free books and gifts will be mine to keep!

316 CIH VDFC
(C-H-R-11/90)

NAME _____
(PLEASE PRINT)

ADDRESS _____ APT. _____

CITY _____

PROV. _____ POSTAL CODE _____

Offer limited to one per household and not valid to current Harlequin Romance® subscribers. All orders subject to approval.

```
AFFIX FREE
VICTORIAN
PICTURE
FRAME
STICKER HERE
```

```
AFFIX FREE
MYSTERY GIFT
STICKER HERE
```

WE EVEN PROVIDE FREE POSTAGE!

It costs you *nothing* to send for your free books — we've paid the postage on the attached reply card. And we'll pick up the postage on your shipment of free books and gifts!

Business Reply Mail

No Postage Stamp
Necessary if Mailed
in Canada

Postage will be paid by

HARLEQUIN READER SERVICE®
P.O. BOX 609
FORT ERIE, ONTARIO
L2A 9Z9

Canada Post
Postes Canada
125

Adam got to his feet, holding Cathy in his arms. His face was set. "How nice of you to give me a say in the matter," he said to Daisy. "But as I think I've pointed out before, I have no intention of moving out."

Louise said, "If you haven't discovered it already, Adam is the most stubborn—"

"It's because he thinks it's unsafe for me to be here by myself," Daisy explained hurriedly.

"If that's the case, I'm sure we could work something out. I could send one of the maids from our place to stay here."

"Will you mind your own business!" Adam roared.

Cathy wriggled down out of his arms. "Uncle Adam, you're shouting again," she admonished.

"You mother would be enough to make a Cistercian monk shout," he snorted.

Daisy giggled, and Louise, with a look that would have toasted bread, said, "I see you think he's funny. Frankly, I don't. I was only trying to help, but if that's all the thanks I get, forget it! As far as I'm concerned the two of you can stew in your own juice."

"That, my dear sister, is precisely what I intend to do." He gave Cathy a hug and pushed her gently toward her mother. "Now take this poor child home to her supper before she starves to death."

"I won't starve," Cathy said stoutly. "I've had lots of biscuits."

"Indeed you have," agreed Adam. He turned to Daisy. "I owe you a packet of custard creams."

Grumbling under her breath, Louise gathered her purse and forced her daughter's arms into the sleeves of a cardigan.

"Oh, Mummy! Must I?" the child protested.

"Don't be silly, Cathy," her mother snapped. "It's cold outside." On the threshold she turned and said to Adam, "Don't forget you *promised* to help with the Disaster Fund Dinner. You can't expect Amy and me to do it all by ourselves."

"Of course not." He went over and opened the door. "Although I'm sure the pair of you would do an excellent job."

"Of course, I'm not sure that Amy's that keen to see you anymore." Louise glared meaningfully.

"In that case I'll stay away. And now will you please get going, or George will be sending out a search party."

Louise regarded him balefully for a second, then she transferred her attention to Daisy. "Are you sure we haven't met before?" she said. "Your face is awfully familiar."

"All beautiful things are familiar," Adam said. He pecked Louise's cheek. "Run along, sis, you know how you hate driving in the mountains at night."

"Yes . . . well, I'll be in touch soon, Adam," she warned. Taking her daughter firmly by the hand, she shut the door behind her.

"I need a drink," said Adam when they heard her car drive away. "I sometimes think the reconciliations with my sister are more wearing than the rows." He went into the kitchen.

Daisy's tawny eyes sparkled with amusement. "If that was a reconciliation I'd hate to see you fighting."

"People tell me it's an awesome sight." He grinned, "Particularly when the five of us are at it."

She paused in the act of turning the oven on. "*Five* of you?"

"Four girls—" he poured generous tots of rum into their glasses "—and me. I was the last child. The longed-for boy."

"The *baby*!" she gurgled, putting the now washed and cleaned fish into a baking pan. "Little Baby Bunting!"

He squinted at her over the rims of his glasses. "That kind of remark can get you into a lot of trouble, angel."

"You must have been dreadfully spoiled."

"Spoiled! Are you joking? Hagridden is what I was. My sainted mother died when I was two and the girls took over. I was bossed around by a bunch of dictatorial females, each determined that I was going to do exactly what she felt was best for me." He handed her a glass of rum and orange. "I started fighting back in my playpen, and I haven't stopped since."

"Don't you love them?" Daisy asked rather wistfully. She'd always longed to be part of a large family.

"Of course I *love* them. I just can't stand to *live* with them. Why do you think I escaped to England as soon as I could?"

"Do they all live in Jamaica?"

"Only two of them. Sheila, the second eldest, and Louise. Louise is only two years older than I am, and she's the bossiest by far. Sheila's married with three kids." He grinned. "All girls. She and her husband run one of my father's plantations near Cockpit Country. It's a nice spot."

Daisy took a tin of peas from her box of supplies and Adam reached over her for the tin opener. His shirt was unbuttoned and she could see the dark hair curling on his chest. She was suddenly filled with an overwhelming desire to nestle against it, to feel its crispness against her cheek.

Jerking away from him, she said abruptly, "That only takes care of two sisters. What happened to the others?"

He didn't answer her immediately, but stood looking at her, an unfathomable expression in his gray eyes. He said finally, "My sister Barbara teaches school in Canada, and you know about the other one. My father's visiting her in Australia."

There was an almost unbearable tension in the little kitchen now, and in an attempt to lessen it Daisy kept up a barrage of questions. Was the sister in Australia married? Had Adam ever visited her there? Did she have only female children as well?

Yes, he said, she was married with two girls, and yes, he'd visited her several times. He travelled a lot in his job.

"And Amy?" Daisy babbled. "Is she another relative?"

For the first time since this strained cross-examination had started she fancied he looked furtive. "No," he said, "she's not a relative—and she's not going to become one, either."

Daisy turned the burner lower under a saucepan. "Does she want to become one, then?"

"I don't know, I never asked her," he replied enigmatically. "Have you timed the fish?"

After this he withdrew into a brooding silence, and Daisy concluded that Amy was a subject he didn't care to discuss. Because of this she found it impossible to think of anything else.

She must be the "Miss Amy" Sarah had spoken of that afternoon at Solitaire. The "Amy" who was helping Louise with the Disaster Fund. When Louise had spoken of her there had been an accusing tone in her voice, although Daisy suspected that that tone was rarely absent when Louise addressed her brother. Nevertheless, this Amy must wield some sort of power over him, since the mere mention of her name drove him to silence.

They spoke little during dinner, and afterward, while Adam did the washing up, Daisy occupied herself with her painting.

She had decided to do a study of palm trees in the classic old-fashioned way, underpainting first in a pale colour, leaving the painted shadows and modelling until the last. She'd done several versions, and now she spread them out on the table and examined them, her fine brows drawn together in a frown.

"They're good," Adam said from behind her.

She jumped. "Oh, you startled me!"

"Sorry, angel." His good nature seemed restored, and he went on. "I like the feeling that the viewer's lying on the ground looking up at the trees."

"The viewer was," she said. "It was hard on the neck, I can tell you."

He put his arms on either side of her and pressed his hands on the table in order to look at the paintings in more detail. She could feel the warmth of his chest against her back, feel his cheek resting against her hair, and she thought she might suffocate in the sudden desire that engulfed her.

To try to hide her emotion she leaned low over the table, as if scanning the paintings for microscopic flaws. "I need to use more ochre," she croaked, "to enhance the suggestion of sunlight."

He lifted his hands from the table and stood upright again, and she was irrationally disappointed to be released from the dangerous circle of his arms. She turned to glance at him over her shoulder. He was contemplating her intently, the expression in his gray eyes unfathomable.

Under this penetrating gaze she started to babble. "I wonder if I should use Japanese paper? Except it's so tricky to use.... I used it once on a seascape and all my waves fell out of the picture. Well, they didn't really *fall*, they sort of squished down into the bottom...like a jelly that won't set. Still, Japanese paper would be nice.... What do you think?"

"I think," he said slowly, "that it was a black day for me when you came to Jamaica. You do more damage than any hurricane ever has. And that's a fact, Daisy Gordon."

CHAPTER SEVEN

DAISY WAS HAVING TROUBLE keeping up with Adam's moods. The man was like a yo-yo. "I fail to see how painting palm trees could damage them," she said finally.

He raked a long-fingered hand through his hair. "As I may have mentioned before," he said, "I have a natural antipathy to matrimony."

She gave a strangled laugh. "Mentioned it! You never stop going on about it."

"That's because I'm naturally—" he groped for a word "—*cautious*."

"You can say that again."

"And because I want to be fair," he said, looking at her intently. "I want you to know exactly where I stand."

He was being downright obscure, and she was losing patience. "Why?" she inquired tartly. "Your feelings about marriage have nothing to do with me."

"You're not a fool. You must be aware of the chemistry between us," he said gruffly. "You're a beautiful woman, and..."

Daisy sat ramrod straight in her chair. The memory of his rejection still smarted. "I seem to remember that you turned me down flat," she said coldly.

He looked at her steadily and she found herself admiring his troubled gray eyes. Hastily she looked away. Gazing into his eyes wasn't the way to keep her cool.

He said, "I explained about that."

"Something about not betraying my trust, wasn't it? I don't recall you mentioning your fear of matrimony, though."

"I didn't understand then what a threat you were," he explained wearily. He gave her a crooked smile that in ordinary circumstances would have touched her heart. "You're the sort of girl who makes a man forget his principles."

That was what one of those damn newspapers had said, and Daisy coloured hotly. "Don't worry. Your principles are perfectly safe," she informed him loftily. "We're *not* having an affair."

"We're not having an affair…yet," he said quickly.

"Let me assure you that there's no chance of it," said Daisy, her eyes glittering like topaz. "You can put your mind at rest."

He gave a groan. "Oh, Daisy! We could be so good together. I know it." He reached out his hand to touch her, but she leaped out of her chair and backed away. "We could have a wonderful, unforgettable affair. But I want to be honest with you. It could never be more than that."

"Honest!" Daisy's voice rang out like the Liberty Bell. "Don't make me laugh, Adam Deverell. You just want your fun and no commitment." Her lips curled. "I had a father like that. It's not a breed of male I admire." In the silence following this statement she could

hear the tree frogs chirping away like mad in the forest outside.

Adam said, "I know you're not the type to sleep around, angel."

True. But would he have thought that if he'd read about her in the papers?

"Just the same," he continued ruefully, "I was hoping you might be interested in making love with me." He reached out and drew her toward him, but she remained stiff in his arms. Unyielding, even when he lightly kissed her hair and said, "You smell as sweet as a child's biscuit."

God knew she wanted to surrender. She did desire him so much. She had since that evening when he dried her hair. Since even before that if she was honest. Nevertheless, she disengaged herself from his embrace and said firmly, "You'll have to go and stay somewhere else, Adam. I can't have you here, breathing down my neck all the time."

"What's the matter, angel? Don't you trust yourself around me?"

He had hit a nerve and she flushed peony pink. "Don't be ridiculous! *You're* the one who's suffering from uncontrollable passion."

"I didn't say it was uncontrollable."

"Just the same—"

"I'm not leaving you here alone, Daisy. Particularly at night. It's not safe." His obstinate jaw jutted.

"I'm not sure it's particularly safe here at night with you steaming in the next room," she told him, standing her ground.

"I've never forced myself on a lady." He smiled. "You're safe until you don't want to be, my angel. And now—" he kissed her lightly on her forehead "—now I'm going to my chaste bed." He paused at his bedroom door and said with a grin, "See you at breakfast. I won't lock my door, in case you change your mind."

She grinned back then, and threw a paintbrush after his retreating figure. It all seemed very lighthearted, except she didn't feel lighthearted at all. She felt unsettled, and out of sorts with the world.

She had known, of course, that the attraction between them was powerful. She had known that it would take very little to get her into his arms, into his bed, into his life. But she also knew that his *life* was the one place he didn't want her. His life included the possibility of a permanent attachment, and Adam had made it quite clear that permanent attachments were not in his scheme of things.

Then why was she wasting time thinking about such an improbable situation? Not that the possibility of an affair with Adam was improbable. Far from it. She would have had to be made of stone not to be aware of the electricity that crackled between them. The delicious sexual tension.

So why didn't she go and knock on his door now, melt into his arms, let herself be lost in a blaze of passion that she felt sure he was more than capable of igniting? She looked over at his door hesitantly. A few steps and her life would be changed forever.

No, it wouldn't! All that would happen would be a brief, exciting affair, and she didn't need that. She was trying to escape from scandal, not dally with some stranger, no matter how attractive he might be. If she felt the need for a man in her life all she had to do was to write to Nigel. Beg his forgiveness for all the trouble she'd caused him, and for disappearing without a word. It might take a while but she knew he'd come around in the end. He just needed coaxing. She knew what he was like.

But she didn't want Nigel. Just *thinking* about Nigel was like drinking water after the most delicious champagne.

Just the same, it wasn't really decent to contemplate popping into bed with a man so soon after breaking her engagement, even if the man in question was the most devastating male she'd ever encountered. And with these moral thoughts to sustain her she packed up her painting gear and made her lonely way to her own room.

To her relief, breakfast the next morning was free from any tension. Adam was cheerful and treated her just as before, so that the easy banter that had become a pattern with them was reestablished, and she relaxed. Perhaps, she thought as she spread jam on her toast, he'd decided that friendship was preferable to an affair. But no. When he passed her knapsack to her he held her close for a moment, and whispered into the curve of her neck, "Another night wasted, angel."

She said primly, "I didn't waste the night. I slept like a log."

"When do you have to go back to England, Daisy?" he asked, letting her go.

She started to tuck her silky hair up into her linen sun hat with fingers that shook a little, for she was still vibrating from his light caress. "I'm due back on December sixth."

"Just two weeks," he said thoughtfully. "It doesn't leave me much time."

She looked up at him, tendrils of glossy hair escaping from under the brim of her hat. "Time for what?"

He gave her a stage villain's exaggerated leer. "To entice you to me bed, me proud beauty!"

"La, sir!" She fluttered her thick lashes. "Would you trick a poor defenceless girl into a fate worse than death?"

"I don't know about defenceless," he remarked in a normal tone. "You defend yourself pretty well with whatever comes to hand, I recall. That statue could have been lethal."

"The fish couldn't," she said, going out into the sunshine.

"The fish had the element of surprise," he said as he followed her out of the villa. "And while we're about it—" he opened the trunk of her car and put her knapsack in "—I'm not sure I like the idea of a fate worse than death. My previous ladies have assured me that they've enjoyed themselves enormously."

"I'm sure they did." She climbed into the driver's seat, slamming the door in a spurt of jealous irritation. "I hope you got them to write references."

"I rely on word of mouth, angel," he drawled. "And, Daisy..." She looked up from switching on the ignition. "You're lovely when you're jealous."

"Jealous? Ha! That'll be the day." She shot away, leaving him grinning.

Like a Cheshire cat, she thought crossly, for this particular piece of tomfoolery had been closer to the truth than she cared to admit.

The thought of him making love to other women was like a thorn in her heart, and this surprised her, for she had never thought of herself as the jealous type. She certainly hadn't been jealous of Nigel. Of course, she knew Nigel well, and she didn't know Adam at all. Not really.

And the odd thing about that, she thought as she negotiated a particularly nasty turn, the odd thing about that was that part of her felt as if she'd known Adam all her life. Which just went to show that sex was a very self-deluding instinct, because of course that was what it was. Just sex. She was quite willing to admit that she fancied Adam physically. Far more than she'd ever fancied her erstwhile fiancé.

Pleased by her excessive honesty, for she wouldn't have admitted such a thing even a week ago, she drove into Devil's Gully and parked the car under a tree.

There weren't as many people around as there had been last night. Most of the men were working and the children were at school. Daisy set up her easel and camp stool and started an all prima watercolour of a shanty set precariously on the side of the hill. Soon she had an audience of three women and several small children, who were more interested in her black enamel spit-box with its tiny pots of paint than in the work in progress.

"You good at that, missus," a plump lady in orange complimented. "You done it a long time?"

"All my life," Daisy told her. She adjusted the small sunshade that was clipped on to her easel to give more shade. "And the name's Daisy."

There was a general exchange of names after this, and then the youngest-looking woman, who had introduced herself as Penny, announced, "That's my cabin you paintin'."

Daisy angled her paper to stop the wet paint running to the bottom. "You must have a great view from there."

"Not bad," Penny agreed.

"'Specially of the sky," interjected the woman in orange, who was known as Matilda. "She ain't got her roof back on yet."

"Gilbert?" asked Daisy, and Penny nodded. "How do you manage when it rains?"

"I got tarpaulin up," said Penny, and then she smiled shyly and Daisy realized that she was very young, much younger than she'd first imagined.

"I thought Adam Deverell was fixing things like that," said Daisy.

"There weren't no hurry to fix my place," Penny explained. "I bin away."

"Chasin' after Bram's daddy," Agnes, the oldest of the trio, volunteered. She looked at the younger girl with scorn. "Not that it did her much good. I could'a told her she was wastin' her time."

"Bram's my little boy," Penny said proudly, scooping up a small child who was crawling around her feet and presenting him for inspection.

He was a beautiful child with strong limbs and eyes like great black stars. "What a poppet!" Daisy exclaimed, holding out her hand to him. "How old is he?"

"Eighteen months," said his mother. "He big for his age. Like his daddy."

Agnes snorted. "Le's hope that's the only thing he inherits from that man."

"Dev ain't so bad," Penny protested.

"Any man what runs away from his 'sponsibilities is bad," Agnes declared.

"Dev, Bram's daddy, he don't want to get married," Penny explained.

"You should'a chose a good man," Matilda commented. "They's plenty on the island."

"We told you all along that Dev was bad news," said Agnes, getting into the act again. "You should never have gone with him."

"I loved him," Penny said quietly.

"Love don't put no food in your belly," Agnes said firmly.

Penny's mouth grew stubborn. "I love Dev, an' he love me," she insisted.

"You should'a chose a good man to love," Matilda repeated.

"You can't choose love," Penny said. "He just come at you any way he like." She appealed to Daisy. "Ain't that right?"

"I'm afraid it is," she agreed. She smiled at the baby, who was leaning out from his mother's arms in an attempt to grab the wet paintbrush. "Can I hold him?" she asked, putting down the brush.

Smiling broadly, Penny put him onto Daisy's lap. He gave a delighted gurgle and lunged for the paint pots, which Daisy managed to move out of his reach. He was difficult to hold because he kept squirming about trying to get at the various delightful things in front of him, but after a bit of a struggle she managed to turn him round. Taking a piece of scrap paper and the pot of red paint, she began to help him make a finger painting.

"What shall we draw?" she asked, dipping his finger into the paint and holding it over the paper. "A horse? Or maybe a doggie?"

But he wanted none of that. "Bram," he declared loudly. "Draw Bram!"

She guided his finger into a wobbly circle, and made two dots for the eyes. "And a big smile," she said, "just like yours."

The baby gave a joyful crow and started scribbling all over the paper, and Daisy laughed and hugged him close, pressing her smooth cheek against his crinkly black curls.

"He's gettin' paint all over your shirt," Penny warned.

Daisy shook her bright head. "All artists get paint on them. Bram's no exception. Of course he's going to get messy."

"He never draw before," his mother told her, "'cept in the dirt."

Daisy looked down at the cheerful little boy. He was barefoot, his clothes, while well worn, were spotless. His satiny skin looked polished he was so clean. Daisy felt a sudden spurt of anger. How *could* a man help to create such a child, and then turn his back on him? Here, warm and solid on her lap, was beautiful living proof of a love shared between a man and a woman, and yet the woman—in this case little more than a girl—had been abandoned and left to carry the full responsibility alone. It reminded Daisy of her father's betrayal.

It also reminded her of Adam's flat statement about marriage. He wanted his fun, too, he'd made no bones about that, and then—goodbye, Daisy! Just like this Dev character and Penny. Well, thank Providence she'd met Penny. Any time she felt herself coming under Adam's spell she'd remind herself of Penny's plight and so arm herself against him.

Reluctantly she gave Bram back to his mother, and the three women went about their business.

"Can I do a painting from your balcony tomorrow?" Daisy called after Penny.

"That would be real *irie*," the girl said with a smile, hitching Bram higher onto her hip. "See you in de light."

In the afternoon Daisy drove down the mountain, searching for some trees that Matilda had assured her had not been badly damaged by the hurricane. It took her longer than she anticipated, for she was unaware that the Jamaican phrase *just aroun' de corner* could mean anything from a quarter of a mile to ten. But she finally found a calabash that still had some of the strange roundish fruit on it, and a thick-trunked ceiba, or cotton tree. She made some preliminary sketches, and then set off for Tamarind Cottage.

Adam's Jeep was already there, and he was sitting on the porch going over a sheaf of papers. He looked unusually smart in white cotton slacks and a pink shirt, his hair combed sleekly for a change. Even his glasses seemed to sparkle.

"You're back early. That's great!" he said when she came up the steps toward him. "You'll be glad to hear the electricity's on at last."

If Daisy didn't seem as pleased by this as he'd hoped, it was because she was repressing the jolt of pleasure she'd experienced when she saw him. She didn't like feeling such a lift every time she laid eyes on him. That spelled danger.

"It means you can have a nice hot bath at last," he went on. "But no wallowing. At least not this afternoon, otherwise we'll be late."

"Late for what?" She took off her hat and shook out her red-gold mane.

"For dinner with my sister Sheila," he informed her.

"Are you certain I'm included in the invitation?" She was not sure she particularly wanted to meet any more of Adam's sisters.

"Of course you are, angel. You're the only reason. She's still angry with me."

She said doubtfully, "I'm not sure...."

"Well, I am. Now, hurry up. It's a long drive and I want you to see some of the country before it gets dark. Interesting foliage and stuff for your paintings," he added temptingly.

"I don't know." Daisy hesitated. It wasn't only the thought of this unknown relative sniping at him. What if she had read anything about Marguerite and recognized her, the way Louise nearly had?

"Don't dither, angel," he chivvied. "The country's really stunning. Besides—" he gave her an oblique look "—I'd enjoy the pleasure of your company."

"All right," she said, smiling.

She remembered that he'd said that his sister Sheila lived near the area of Jamaica known as Cockpit Country, which was quite different from the Blue Mountains. And that, she told herself as she went into the house, was why he'd managed to persuade her to change her mind.

She had a quick bath and washed her hair. At last, she could use her hair dryer. Then she put on a dress for the first time in weeks.

It was an old dress, one she'd had for years, but it was one of her favourites. A loose shift, which she wore pulled in at the waist with a wide belt. Its attraction for her was the material, a rough woven cotton, and the colour, which was like faded nasturtiums.

She let her hair flow loosely over her shoulders, a silken bell, only slightly paler than her dress. Slipping her narrow feet into flat Mexican-style sandals, she was gratified to see that her feet were beginning to turn a pale gold. Her milky skin would never tan, but it would be nice to show off a small glow when she went home, even if it was only on her feet.

Home. She paused in the act of putting on a plaited straw bracelet. She hadn't thought of Trebethwick Cove in weeks. Her life before coming to Jamaica, before meeting Adam, seemed years away, but in two weeks she'd be back in England. And how was that going to feel? Would the villagers still eye her disapprovingly?

Of course she didn't have to stay in Trebethwick Cove. She could leave Cornwall. Go and live in London. Except that London was expensive and she'd have to be careful about money in the future. Not that she was unused to thrift, but until last month she had believed her future was secure with Nigel.

Well, it wasn't secure any longer. She was a freelance artist, alone in the world, and her life was going to be uncertain at best. No more trips to exotic Caribbean islands. No more rented cars and mountain villas. Well, that was no hardship. Trips abroad and rented villas hadn't figured prominently in her life in the past. She wasn't going to fall apart at the thought of a little austerity in the future.

So why did the future suddenly look so gray? So empty?

She leaned forward to stare at her reflection in the mirror as if seeking the answer there. But she already knew the answer in her heart.

Once she'd boarded the plane back to England, Adam would be out of her life forever. Her heart beat like a dirge. Alone...alone...alone.

CHAPTER EIGHT

"YOU'D THINK THAT AFTER being brought up with four sisters I would have learnt that women take a long time in the bathroom," Adam said when she joined him. Getting to his feet, he draped the light wool shawl she was carrying around her shoulders. "Not that you really need it, angel," he said, "but it gives me an excuse to touch you."

His hands were very gentle, and she thought, *If Adam had been my fiancé instead of Nigel, I bet he would have stood by me.*

Or would he? She didn't really know him that well and men were strange creatures; there was no telling how they might react. She could quite understand that it was no small matter reading about the woman you'd planned to marry, seeing her name linked with a man who was not only old enough to be her father but married as well.

Would Adam believe her if she told him the truth? Perhaps, but it wasn't something she was willing to risk. Besides, under the circumstances it seemed pointless to tell him. It was not as if they had a future together.

One thing she did know: Adam wouldn't have given a hoot about her reputation, much less his own. And if he had accepted her explanation he would have fought for her. He'd have dealt with the press and got that retraction printed, and heaven help Peggy Matheson if she'd been foolish enough to try to stop him.

It would have been nice, Daisy thought wistfully, to have had Adam's strength to lean on. But such day-dreaming was a waste of time. The way Adam felt about marriage, she had about as much chance of being engaged to him as being engaged to...to Prince Charles.

"Are you all right?" he asked when they were sitting in the Jeep.

She smiled. "Just recovering from the rush. You may not believe it, but I did hurry."

"You were certainly worth waiting for. You look like a lovely sunset."

"You mean I'm slowly sinking in the west?"

His gray eyes regarded her thoughtfully. "If there's any sinking it will be into my arms," he said.

She couldn't hold his gaze. Smoothing her skirt over her long legs, she said. "Shouldn't we be off? It'll start getting dark in a couple of hours."

"You can't keep on evading me, Daisy," he said quietly, starting the engine and backing the Jeep onto the road. "It's simply not in the cards."

Maybe she couldn't, but it wasn't quite that simple. She wasn't the type to enjoy brief affairs, let alone with a man like Adam. She had already experienced a hint of the kind of passion he could stir in her. He would burn her to a cinder.

And when she had waved the last goodbye and returned home, what then? It was no good telling herself that they would continue the affair in England. In England she was more likely to be recognized as the notorious Marguerite Gordon. Not the sort of woman a successful young architect needed at his side. No, anything between her and Adam would be a lovely interlude. Short and very sweet, and then she would be left alone again, and she couldn't face that. There had been too many abandonments in her life.

They left Spanish Town behind and drove swiftly toward Mandeville and the sleepy little backwater of Wrenworth where Sheila and her husband lived.

As they approached Mandeville the land started to rise, and soon they were skirting deep valleys. The horizon was ringed with purple hills, and ahead Daisy could see the tousled heads of coconut palms, and sometimes faint blue wisps of plantation fires that rose from the valley below.

When the sun was turning to dusty gold they left the main road and drove down toward a lush valley. Here the shadows were deep and cool. Cattle grazed peacefully, and hawks hovered on the air currents above them.

"What a lovely island Jamaica is," Daisy exclaimed. "I don't know how you can bear to live anywhere else."

Adam gave her a brief glance. The wind had ruffled his dark hair again, but he still looked remarkably well groomed. A far cry from the dirty stranger who had fallen into her life so dramatically two weeks

before. There was a gold signet ring on his little finger that she hadn't noticed before, and the hefty
workmanlike watch he generally wore had been replaced by a wafer-thin gold one.

"That's my sisters' refrain," he said, "and I don't
need another voice added to the chorus." They had
reached the bottom of the hill now, and he pressed
down hard on the accelerator, sending a rain of peb-
bles spurting under the wheels of the Jeep.

"Sheila and Louise refuse to admit that I've done
very well for myself in England," he said tersely.
"They also refuse to admit that I'm in Jamaica for a
good part of each year. So you lay off, Daisy. Understand?"

"I wasn't laying *on*," she said mildly. "It was a
general statement. No need to take offence."

"There is," he said, "when I think you might be
joining their ranks."

"I only know one of them," she pointed out, "and
I suspect that the only thing she'd want me to join is
the French Foreign Legion."

"Louise always was as thick as a plank."

Daisy wondered if Louise would be there tonight,
and hoped not. She didn't feel up to dealing with two
Deverell females at once. "What is Cockpit Country
exactly?" she asked Adam, deciding that it was safer
to talk about the scenery.

"The cockpits are small hills pocked with, uh,
glades I suppose you'd call them. They're hard to
reach. You have to be prepared to climb escarpments

of limestone, fight your way through liana. But it's worth the sweat because they're very beautiful.''

"I must see one before I go." She turned in her seat, huge eyes shining.

He answered firmly, "Not by yourself, Daisy. People have been known to wander in them for days without finding a way out."

"But I must see them. If they're so enclosed it's possible that Gilbert didn't do as much harm there as on the higher ground. There must be plants there I haven't seen."

"I'll try and find the time to take you," said Adam, "but you must promise me, Daisy. No little explorations on your own. It's too dangerous."

She made a little noise in the back of her throat, which could have been taken for assent, but was made simply because she didn't want him nagging at her. She was a truthful girl and she wasn't about to make a promise she wasn't prepared to keep.

He said, "That's settled then."

She murmured softly, "Is it?" And then they swung into the drive of a handsome old house that was sitting hidden in a grove of trees.

A large black Labrador bounded toward them, barking. "Don't let Dulcie frighten you," said Adam. "She looks fierce, but actually she can hardly bring herself to bite a bone."

Daisy said, "I like dogs," and as if she understood, Dulcie stopped barking and began prancing around them and generally showing off.

"Idiot!" said Adam, patting the ecstatic dog, who promptly lay down on her back. "Sheila firmly believes that she's a guard dog," he told Daisy, "but everyone for miles around knows that Dulcie's a total failure. Fortunately she makes a lot of noise, and burglars don't like that."

The front door opened and a tall, dark-haired woman came out. "There you are!" she said. "I was beginning to wonder." She gave Daisy a brief but thorough once-over. "You must be Adam's new friend. I've heard a lot about you."

And I bet I know from whom, thought Daisy, smiling sweetly as Adam introduced his sister. After a moment's hesitation Sheila gave Daisy a chilly smile in return and shook hands.

Sheila West was a handsome woman of thirty-nine, with curly hair like her brother's and the same keen gray eyes. Taller than Louise, she was not as blatantly hostile as her younger sister had been. Nevertheless, her manner was cool, and Daisy knew she was being judged every step of the way.

"Would you like to see the garden before the light goes?" Sheila asked. "Adam tells me you're interested in flowers."

Daisy said she would, very much.

Sheila turned to her brother. "Why don't you go in and find Phil? He wants to ask your advice about an extension on the beach house." Adam didn't move. "Go on, Adam. I'd like to talk to Daisy without you breathing down my neck."

"Would you?" said Adam.

"Phil will give you a rum ahead of the others," Sheila wheedled.

"I'm hardly an alcoholic gasping for a drink," Adam replied. He grasped Daisy's arm. "Come on, angel, let's take in the garden before the sun sets."

"You've probably discovered that my little brother is stubborn as a mule," said Sheila, looking distinctly irritated.

"I'm pretty stubborn myself," Daisy told her, thinking how funny it was to hear Adam described as "little." Daisy and his sister were both tall women, but he stood a head higher then both of them.

Sheila started to point out some of the garden's salient features. "Of course it was knocked about quite a bit in the hurricane," she said, "but the tulip tree's in not bad shape, and my hibiscus hedge was hardly touched."

Even in its damaged condition it was a lovely garden, and Daisy didn't find it difficult to be complimentary. But she was very aware of Sheila's cool appraising stare, which made it difficult to relax. She knew it was possible that Sheila had read that magazine article two weeks ago, and recognized her.

"It's a very large garden," Daisy babbled in her nervousness. "It must take a lot of work."

"I wouldn't know about that," Sheila replied. "We employ three gardeners to deal with it."

"My father was a gardener," Daisy told her, "so I understand the kind of work involved."

"What about your mother? Was she a gardener, too?" Sheila drawled.

Daisy's firm chin tilted combatively. "She was a housekeeper, as a matter of fact."

"Like Aunt Maureen," Adam said. He smiled down at Daisy. "Our paternal uncle married his housekeeper. She was from Ireland, and marrying her was the best day's work he ever did. Mind you, he got flak from some of the Deverell clan, but once they realized what a jewel he'd managed to capture they soon shut up."

"That's a switch," said Sheila acidly, "hearing you defend the married state."

"I'm not defending the married state per se," he said, "just Uncle Arthur's choice."

She gave a forced laugh. "This must be very boring for Daisy, hearing us argue about our relatives."

"I wouldn't want Daisy to get the impression that we're all hopeless snobs," he said.

Daisy, who had no wish to witness a family row, simply stood still. "What an enormous tree!" she hastily interrupted.

They were standing by a huge tree whose trunk was so smooth it looked as if it were made of stone. There was a niche at the base of it deep enough to shelter a man.

"Wow! You could *live* in here," she babbled on, stepping inside it.

"Remember when Amy hid in there, Adam?" Sheila asked. She said to Daisy, "It was Adam's sixteenth birthday party and Amy wanted to tease him." Her eyes gleamed in the dusk like a cat's. "It took him an hour to find her, and when he did he kissed her for the first time."

"It wasn't the first time, actually," Adam corrected her. "If you're going to bore us with ancient history you should at least get your facts straight."

"It wasn't the last time, either," his sister snapped.

Adam gave her a measured look, and said firmly, "No. The last time was several years later."

"The light's gone," announced Sheila, although it was barely dusk. "The others will wonder what's happened to us. Let's go inside."

The house was as impressive inside as it was seen from the garden. It had housed three generations of Deverells. Adam's father had only moved out to live at Solitaire Farm when Sheila's family had started to grow.

Daisy was ushered into a large square room that seemed to be filled with people. There were actually eight other guests present, but when they came in and Sheila announced Daisy's name all conversation stopped and all eyes were trained on the newcomer.

Daisy's stomach began to churn. What if someone realized who she really was? What would Adam think of her, when he learned of her deception? The evening was going to be a disaster.

But her fears proved to be groundless. Sheila's genial husband, Philip, thrust a large glass of rum and orange juice into her hand, saying, "I don't know what it is about that brother-in-law of mine, but he always seems to capture the prettiest girls on the island." It was clear Philip hadn't recognized her as

Marguerite. She was no more to him than another of Adam's ladies.

Philip introduced her to the company at large, and Daisy recognized Russel Hurst, Adam's bank manager, among the guests. He grinned at her like an old friend, and came over with his wife.

Gloria Hurst was a beauty, with skin the color of strong coffee and eyes like black velvet. "Well, for once Russel wasn't exaggerating," she said. "He told me Adam had rented the villa to a girl who was a knockout, and he was right."

"You don't know just how much of a knockout," said Adam. Coming and putting his arm across Daisy's shoulders, he proceeded to tell them about the night she'd laid him out with the statue.

Everybody laughed. Then one of the women, who had just returned from a visit to New York, mentioned the name of a new British artist whose work was causing quite a stir there, and Daisy got involved in a friendly discussion on the pros and cons of modern art, and began to enjoy herself.

Apart from Sheila, everyone seemed friendly, and nobody looked at her with the faintly puzzled air of people trying to place where they'd seen her before. It really did look as if the news story was dead and forgotten and she could start living normally again.

They ate in a formal dining room, and were served by two maids. The food was delicious, and Daisy ate things she'd only read about before, like akee, rice and breadfruit, and a wonderful pudding called Matrimony, which was a blend of orange and star apple slices in cream.

She grinned across the table at Adam, who was accepting a second helping from one of the smiling maids. "I'm surprised you dare to eat a sweet with a name like that."

"What's in a name, angel?" he said, spooning up the gleaming fruit. "Besides, I'm learning that life isn't quite so cut-and-dried as I thought."

After coffee, the Deverells' Blue Mountain blend, Gloria decided to teach Daisy to "speak proper Jamaican."

"*Kiss me neck,* girl, you can't live hee an' not speak the language!" she insisted.

"I'm not going to be living here much longer." Daisy smiled.

"Adam won't let you leave," Gloria said, shaking her head emphatically. "No way!"

"It's got nothing to do with Adam," declared Daisy. "I have a return ticket."

With a graceful hand Gloria waved aside this consideration. "Details! He won't let an airplane ticket rob him of the most important thing in his life."

"Oh, come on, Gloria!" protested Daisy. "He may... fancy me, but I'm hardly the most important thing in his life." Then she added, "Even if I was, there wouldn't be any future in it, would there?"

"You mean because he doesn't want to get married?" Gloria gave a hoot of laughter. "When has that ever made a difference?"

"Well, it's not my style to drag any man protesting to the altar."

"You wouldn't have to drag, honey," Gloria declared, giving another hoot of laughter. "The man's in love with you. All you have to do is sit back and he'll wind up leading the way."

Sheila called across the room. "May we share the joke?"

"No joke." Gloria winked at Daisy. "We were just discussing human nature."

"It *sounded* like a joke," insisted Sheila, coming over to them. "Is human nature so amusing?"

She eyed Daisy suspiciously, then turned to the other woman. "We have to have a meeting with Amy soon," she said, "to organize the Disaster Fund Dinner. We need ideas for door prizes."

She didn't exactly turn her back on Daisy, but she managed to make it quite clear that Daisy was an outsider. "It's too bad Amy couldn't be here this evening," Sheila said to Gloria now. *Instead of me, she means,* thought Daisy.

"We could have discussed it," Sheila went on, "thrown a few ideas around."

Fed up with Sheila and her bad manners, Daisy moved away to examine a framed antique map of the island. But she found it hard to concentrate on the faded squiggles and drawings of strange creatures.

She found Gloria's remarks about Adam disturbing. Of course it wasn't true. Gloria had been simply playing the fool. Adam wasn't in love with her. He was sexually attracted to her, which was quite different.

And there was no denying that she was similarly attracted to him. Every time he touched her she felt as if her bones might melt.

As if he sensed her thoughts, Adam, who had been standing at the open French doors talking to his brother-in-law, came over to where Daisy was standing and gently touched her cheek. It was the lightest caress, but she felt her cheek tingle with pleasure.

"You all right, angel?" he asked. "You look a little lonely."

"Just a little tired," she answered brightly.

He scrutinized her over the top of his glasses. "You sure you're okay?"

"Of course!" She spoke more sharply than she intended, unnerved by his perception.

"We'll be going home soon," he told her.

"Whenever you want." She was now anxious to leave. She'd had enough jokes about love and marriage.

"Adam!" Sheila's voice cut across the room. "Gloria and I are having an argument about the door prizes for the Disaster Fund Dinner. Come and give us your opinion."

Daisy's instinct was to drift over toward the other guests, but Adam took her firmly by the hand, and together they went over to the two women.

"Amy suggested that Solitaire Farm should donate a sack of coffee beans as a door prize," Sheila said, looking through Daisy as if she were a pane of glass, "but Gloria's not keen."

"It's coals to Newcastle," Gloria complained. "Heck! We can buy coffee beans in the market."

Sheila said shortly, "Not since the hurricane, you can't. Coffee's very scarce."

"Just the same," said Gloria, "you need something out of the ordinary for a door prize."

"Is Amy still going to donate her Victorian fire screen?" asked Adam. "That's out of the ordinary, surely."

"She's had second thoughts."

Gloria raised an ironic eyebrow, and Sheila said swiftly, "I don't blame her. It really was much too generous."

"Door prizes are pretty run-of-the-mill, if you ask me," declared Adam. "Why not do something more original? Why not hold an auction?"

He looked down at Daisy. "See if you can talk Daisy into donating one of her pictures. That should raise more money than a sack of coffee beans."

Daisy and Sheila said simultaneously, "I don't think—"

But Gloria talked them down. "That's not a bad idea. Art always sells well."

"That depends, doesn't it," said Sheila briskly. "I mean...we don't know what kind of pictures she paints."

"Afraid she might specialize in pornography?" Adam asked with deceptive blandness. Behind the horn-rimmed glasses his eyes were granite hard.

"Don't be silly, Adam," Sheila blustered. "It's just that...that I'm not sure that an auction..."

"Well, I am," Gloria declared. "And if Adam thinks Daisy's stuff is good, that's enough for me." She said to Daisy, "That's assuming, of course, that you're willing to donate a picture."

Daisy nodded her head, her bright hair glittering in the lamplight. "Yes, of course. But don't you think you should see my work before you accept?"

"That's easily arranged," said Adam, taking charge. "I can bring any pictures Daisy might be willing to donate to your place tomorrow evening, Gloria." Gloria agreed that that was just fine.

"Not fine at all," Sheila said. "I'm not sure I can manage tomorrow evening. And what about Amy? And Louise?"

"I'll phone them tomorrow," Gloria volunteered. "If they can both come we won't need you, Sheila. We'll have enough to carry a vote."

And that was that. Sheila had lived through enough battles with her brother to know when she was beaten.

Gloria, who didn't believe in wasting time, gathered the guests together and asked them what they thought of the idea of auctioning a painting in aid of the Disaster Fund.

Their enthusiasm was flattering, and soon they were firing questions at Daisy, asking what sort of things did she paint? Did she do portraits? What medium did she work in?

She did her best to answer, but this sudden interest in her work was rather overpowering. She was grateful when Adam said it was time they were leaving.

"I'm sorry to pry you away from your fans, angel," he said, smiling, "but it's a long drive."

"It's too bad of you, Adam," one of the women complained. "I had no idea Daisy was a painter, and you know I collect art. I can't wait to see her work."

"You'll find it's worth the wait," he promised, putting his arm around Daisy's waist. "Daisy Gordon is a name you're going to be hearing a great deal of in the future."

"That's about the best credential you could get," the woman's husband told Daisy. "Adam's a connoisseur. Have you seen his collection of French Impressionists?"

"N...no," she answered, startled.

"You haven't been to his home in England, then?" asked the man. Daisy shook her head. "It's quite something, I assure you," he went on. "You'll be impressed."

Sheila hustled them away after this, grumbling that they'd said they were going so surely they should *go*. "Adam and his infatuations!" she grumbled, softly enough to be inaudible to her brother.

On the porch Adam remembered that he'd left behind some plans his brother-in-law wanted him to take with him. "I'll just be a minute, Daisy!" he said, and went back into the house.

The sky was like a vast bowl of black velvet scattered with enormous, diamond-bright stars. A three-quarter moon lay on its side above a bank of silver-edged cloud, and a bush of bougainvillea that was just coming into bloom rustled in the darkness.

Daisy took a deep breath of soft air, and then nearly jumped out of her skin when Sheila came snarling out of the shadows.

"You may have succeeded in dazzling Adam," she hissed, "but don't think that the rest of his family is so easily fooled."

Daisy's heart gave a sickening lurch. Was she found out after all? "I haven't the faintest idea what you're talking about," she croaked.

"Do you think I don't know an opportunist when I see one?" Sheila snorted.

"Opportunist?"

"What would you call it?"

Daisy started to breathe a little easier now that she realized her true identity wasn't in question. "I think you must be mad," she said. "I don't know what you're talking about."

"Don't you? I suppose you had no idea that my brother has enormous influence in the art world. Or that he's very rich." She brought her face close to Daisy's. "Well, I just want to warn you. Louise and I . . . we've got our eye on you."

"Your collective eye? Or one each?" Daisy smiled.

"You'll laugh on the other side of your face if we catch you up to any tricks," warned Sheila. Then she suddenly pulled her mouth into a parody of a smile and said, "I'm *so* looking forward to seeing your pictures tomorrow," as Adam came out of the house.

CHAPTER NINE

DRIVING AWAY IN THE JEEP Daisy began to wonder if that nasty little scene with Sheila had been a figment of her imagination. Maybe the change in altitude was giving her hallucinations.

After Adam had joined them his sister hadn't been exactly the soul of affability, but there had been no hint of the venom that had spilled out of her just seconds before. *Maybe I'm too tired to see things properly,* thought Daisy, yawning like a beautiful tawny cat, her white teeth gleaming in the dark.

"Tired, angel?" asked Adam.

She nodded sleepily. "Mmm!"

"I'm afraid the Jeep isn't the best place for a nap, and the seats are so far apart I can't offer you my shoulder as a pillow."

Just as well, thought Daisy. From Sheila's warped point of view even shaking hands with Adam would be tantamount to seducing him. Using his shoulder as a pillow would have felt like a major crime.

She shifted in her seat in an attempt to wake herself up and said, "Do you really think my pictures are good enough to auction, or were you just being kind?"

"You should know me better than that, angel."

"I suppose I should," she agreed, yawning.

He said casually, "That chap who taught you painting..."

She was instantly alert. "What about him?"

"I was just thinking, he may have done wonders with your technique, but he did a rotten job on your self-confidence. You're good, Daisy. It's time you realized it, and started blowing your own horn for a change."

"Just the same, I'll look a right idiot if nobody bids."

"They'll bid," he promised. "But not on the one you did of the mountains in the mist."

She gave a little splutter of surprise. "Why ever not? I think that's my best."

He took his eyes briefly from the road ahead to glance at her. "That's mine, angel, and I'm willing to pay a good price for it."

Pleased, she said, "You don't have to pay a good price for it. I'll let you have it cheap."

"Daisy, Daisy!" He shook his head in mock despair. "You'll never make your fortune if you carry on like that. I've got plenty of money. Take advantage of it."

"That's something I'm not very good at," she said, although she was sure Sheila wouldn't agree.

It was the first time he had mentioned having money, and the first time she'd thought of him as being rich. He certainly hadn't looked rich during his stay at the villa. But of course he'd been helping to clear landslides, he'd hardly have been wearing silk suits and ties.

Now that she thought about it, she realized that she'd been stupid not to have seen right away that the Deverells were wealthy. They owned enormous tracts of land and beautiful houses, all part of the trappings of the well-to-do, and Adam had said he spent a good deal of each year in Jamaica. You couldn't do that on a shoestring budget, so perhaps it was understandable that Sheila and Louise were so antagonistic. Any woman who was not part of their set would be suspect, particularly if she happened to be a penniless artist.

Just the same, thought Daisy wearily, there had been no reason for Sheila to behave like that. Adam was a grown man; it was ludicrous, his sisters treating him like a child. She stifled another yawn. She was too tired to think about it anymore. Tomorrow she'd work extra hard and clear her mind of all this emotional debris.

But the next morning was overcast. Not a great day for painting. Still, she set off after breakfast, remembering that she had a date with Penny. In any case she wanted to get away from the villa. Away from the temptation of being close to Adam.

Last night when they got back he had taken her into his arms and sung softly, "'Daisy, Daisy, give me your answer do.'"

She had laughed and pulled herself free. "You know the answer, Adam. It's 'No, thank you very much.'"

But in her heart it had been, "Yes, please!" Only the recollection of Sheila's furious face had held her back.

And this morning the physical chemistry between them was so powerful that she was unable to concentrate. She was going to have to do something about it. But what? That was the problem.

THE MOUNTAINS AROUND Devil's Gully were shrouded in mist, and by the time she'd climbed up to the shack a light rain was falling.

She found Penny standing precariously on top of a rickety table trying to secure her tarpaulin ceiling. "I'll get us a glass o' juice when I get this t'ing fixed right," she promised.

"Let me try. I'm taller than you," said Daisy, unwinding Bram's clutching arms and handing him to his mother.

She pulled and tugged at the flapping sheets. "I'm afraid that's the best I can do," she said, clambering down again. They scanned the drooping material dubiously. "It doesn't look very waterproof."

Penny said, "It never did work too well. Never has from the start."

Daisy looked around the one-room shanty. Apart from the table there was a battered chair and an iron bedstead that had seen better days. The single uncovered pillow was partially hidden by a worn blanket. The one thing that looked new was a green plastic basin and a large packet of soap powder. The whole place was damp.

"The fire went out, or I'd make us a cup o' coffee," Penny said, handing her guest a plastic cup of orange juice. She didn't pour any for herself or Bram, and Daisy had a nasty suspicion that there wasn't enough to go around.

"You can't stay here, Penny," she blurted, "not without a proper roof."

"Rainy season's nearly over," the girl commented stoutly.

"It's never over in the mountains," Daisy said. "And what about Bram?"

Penny looked sheepish. "He do catch cold sometimes."

"You see! I'm surprised at Adam neglecting you like this."

"He didn't." Penny looked shamefaced. "He wanted to fix the roof an' I wouldn't let him."

"Why ever not? It wasn't anything to do with money, was it?"

"Rhaatid" exclaimed Penny. "Adam Deverell, he don't *charge* people. No—" she played with the skirt of her cotton dress "—I jes' thought if Dev heard we ain't got no roof . . . he might come an' fix it."

"Dev. That's Bram's father, isn't it?" said Daisy, searching her memory. Penny nodded. "Oh, Penny! It's been eight weeks since Gilbert. Don't you think, if Dev was coming, he would have come by now?"

"I guess." She looked so forlorn, Daisy went and put her arms around her.

"Listen, I've got an idea. I'll speak to Adam, get him to do your roof right away, and in the meantime, you and Bram can come and stay with me."

Penny's brown eyes opened wide. "At Tamarind Cottage?"

"That's right! It'll be fun for me to have you both, and you'll have a chance to dry yourselves out."

Penny hesitated. "But . . . Mr. Adam, what will he say?"

"Why, nothing!" Daisy replied, with a great deal more conviction than she felt. "He'll be delighted that I've got company. He's only been staying on because he doesn't want me to be alone there."

"Well, if you're sure," said Penny, looking hopeful.

"Of course I'm sure. Come on! There isn't any view today, so I can't paint. Let's pack up your things before the rain gets heavier. We've got hot water at the villa now," she added as further inducement.

It didn't take long to tie Penny's meagre belongings into a bundle. On the way out she picked up a saucepan and a battered wooden spoon.

"I've got plenty of pots and pans," Daisy told her.

"This is for Bram," Penny explained, and it occurred to Daisy that this was probably the only toy the little boy owned.

Penny insisted on writing a note and pinning it on the door. "So folks will know where I gone," she said, and then she mumbled, "Dev, too, if he come."

When Penny was settled in the passenger seat, Daisy put Bram, who was wrapped in a piece of sacking to keep off the rain, onto her lap. "Ber-ber-ber," he chortled gleefully, hitting his chubby fists on the dashboard.

"He thinks he in a bus," said his mother fondly. "He ain't never been in a car before."

"We'll have to take some drives while you're staying at the villa," said Daisy, wondering if she could manage to buy Bram some toys during one of them. She'd have to look at her budget.

"This real *irie* of you, Daisy," said Penny shyly, and Daisy smiled and told her it was nothing.

She was all too aware that her hospitable gesture was not wholly altruistic. Since there were only two bedrooms at Tamarind Cottage Adam would have to move out, and the problem of the sexual electricity that existed between them would be gone. Well, not exactly gone; even when he wasn't around she still desired him. But if he wasn't lying just across the hall from her every night, the overwhelming temptation to tap on his door or invite him into her room was removed.

Now all that remained was to tell Adam, and she wasn't looking forward to that. She'd have to play it by ear and hope that he wouldn't make a fuss. *After all,* she thought in a self-righteous attempt to plump up her courage, *I'm the one who's renting the villa. Adam's nothing more than... than a squatter!*

Her squatter returned late that afternoon, covered in plaster dust and in tearing spirits. Daisy was taking a short breather from the day's activities. Penny had become enraptured with the hot water on tap and had proceeded to wash everything she could lay her hands on, finishing with herself and her son. The villa was festooned with lines of laundry.

"Hey! Who do we have here?" said Adam, picking up Bram and swinging him into the air.

Daisy looked up from cutting out squares of cardboard for an alphabet she had decided to make for the child. The moment she'd heard Adam's Jeep drive up her mouth had gone dry and her grip on the scissors had weakened.

"I've got visitors," she said unnecessarily.

"I gathered that." He put the gurgling baby back into the playpen the women had manufactured out of a large cardboard box. "Did you kidnap him? Or did he just amble up by himself?"

"His mother's taking a nap," Daisy told him.

Adam grinned. "Not for long!" he said, because at that moment Bram started beating on his saucepan with the wooden spoon.

"Bram! No, sweetie!" exclaimed Daisy, taking the saucepan and spoon away. Bram started bellowing like a wounded buffalo.

"Hey, young fellow!" said Adam, scooping him up again. "None of that. You'll break the lady's eardrums."

After a few seconds Bram's roars subsided, he hiccoughed a couple of times and then made a grab for Adam's glasses. "Active little tyke, isn't he?" remarked Adam, tucking the baby under his arm. He looked around at the drying laundry. "Did he do the washing, too?"

Daisy giggled. "Penny did it. She washed everything in sight."

"Including my clean shirts, by the look of it. Lilly will be thrilled."

"Adam! I've asked them to stay," said Daisy in a rush. "Penny and Bram. It's raining, and their shack is so damp and cold and Penny doesn't have a proper roof since the hurricane." She took a deep breath. "I've given them your room."

He hitched Bram into a more comfortable position. "And where do I go, angel? Do I move in with you?"

"No, Adam," she said quietly, "you don't."

She looked down at her drawings, pretending to study the card that read "B is for breadfruit," surprised at the pain this was causing her.

She expected him to object. It was a sudden eviction, and she could understand any indignation he might feel. But he simply said, "If that's the way you want it, Daisy," and put Bram back in his cardboard box.

His expression became shuttered, and she felt a pang of guilt because she was sure she had hurt him. She started to babble, "Their place is really damp, Adam, it's not good for the baby. Penny says he gets a lot of colds. I couldn't let him stay there. As soon as their roof's fixed they'll move back. It's not for long."

His eyes were blank. "It's all right, Daisy, I understand."

She muttered, "I hope so," and lapsed into silence.

"When Penny's had her nap I'll pack up my clothes," he said, and he started collecting his papers and bundling them into a neat pile. Then he went into the bathroom and got his sponge bag and shaving kit, as if he was suddenly eager to be off.

She couldn't bear watching him methodically getting ready to clear out of her life like this. She exclaimed, "You don't have to move out this minute!"

"No point putting if off, angel. Besides—" he gave his lopsided grin "—junior there would make short work of my blueprints once he got his little paws on them."

"I wouldn't let him." She looked at Bram, who was now contentedly gnawing on the side of his box. "In any case, he seems to have other interests."

"For the time being. But once he's eaten his way out of there, there's no telling where he'll attack next."

"You will stay for dinner, won't you?" said Daisy, cursing herself for sounding plaintive.

He looked at her as coolly as a solicitor assessing a new client. "Thanks, but I don't think I will. I have to be at the Hursts' at eight with those pictures you promised."

Oh Lord! She'd forgotten all about her donation to the Disaster Fund. Hastily she picked up her portfolio and searched through it. "Would these do?" She held out three of her finished pieces.

"Very generous." He took two pieces of the cardboard she was using for Bram's alphabet and put the pictures between them. He didn't suggest that she come with him to Russel and Gloria's, and she was glad about that. It was never a good idea to have the artist present. But she knew perfectly well that that was not the reason why she felt a craven sense of relief.

The reason was Amy Preston, the girl Adam's sisters had chosen for him. She might be at the Hursts' and Daisy didn't want to meet her. Not tonight. Not ever.

"Where will you stay?" she asked, as casually as she could . . . not that it was really any of her business.

"For the time being I'll go to Solitaire."

How overjoyed Lilly would be to have him back under the family roof. *And the irony is,* Daisy thought, *it's me she has to thank for it. Talk about cutting off your nose to spite your face!*

"Then I'll move back into the beach house," he went on. "It's nearly ready."

"And the weather's so nice . . . I mean for the beach," she chattered. "The swimming should be great now." She couldn't think of anything sensible to say, except, *Don't go, Adam. Please don't go.* And she couldn't say that.

He didn't try to make conversation, and so her babbling died away. An uncomfortable silence reigned until Penny woke up and Adam went into the bedroom to collect his things, and the two girls started concocting dinner from Daisy's dwindling supply of tins and packets.

Eventually he came out of the bedroom, carrying his suitcase. How Daisy hated that case. It spelled the end of what had turned into a very happy time for her.

To counteract this horrible sense of loss she became very businesslike.

"Some of this stuff is yours," she called briskly from the kitchen recess. "This tin of ham, and these water biscuits. I'll put them in a bag for you, shall I?"

"Don't be idiotic," he snapped.

She was horrified to discover that she was close to tears. Goodbyes always affected her this way, and this one seemed particularly hard to take. *Don't be a fool,* she told herself. *He's not going far. He'll still be on the island. Pull yourself together.*

"I don't think I should eat your food," she said gruffly. "It doesn't seem right."

"Don't eat it then." He glared from behind his glasses. "Throw it in the sea. Burn it. But for heaven's sake stop behaving like a provincial landlady."

Daisy thrust the tin of ham back in the cupboard and, picking up the wooden spoon, began to energetically stir the pan of spaghetti sauce, two bright spots of colour on her cheeks.

She was grateful to Adam, because she didn't feel like crying anymore. Not over him. Not on your life! He'd been so charming these past few weeks, she'd forgotten what a pain he could be. Well, it was fortunate he'd reverted to type before she'd made a complete fool of herself.

"See you around," she said offhandedly.

And he said, "Maybe," nodded at Penny and took himself and his belongings out to the Jeep.

"He sure seems *rhaatid*," ventured Penny. "I don't think he's pleased we come."

"Rubbish!" Daisy said firmly. Then she added, "It doesn't matter whether he's pleased or not."

Penny didn't seem convinced. "Jes' the same..."

"Please don't fuss about it, Penny." The Jeep roared away with a squeal of tires. "There, he's gone." She forced a smile. "Now we can have a nice relaxed supper to celebrate your arrival. Let's have some wine, shall we?"

But Penny didn't drink, and since Daisy didn't fancy drinking alone, the wine remained unopened.

Bram managed to shatter any hopes of a relaxed meal by dumping his bowl of spaghetti and tomato sauce on the floor and spending the rest of the dinner hour screaming his head off. By the time Daisy served coffee she was almost tempted to regret her impetuous invitation.

After they had washed up, Penny attempted to put Bram to bed while Daisy returned to painting the alphabet. It was a very still night with hardly a breath of wind, and for the first time since she'd come here, Daisy was aware of the loneliness of the place. If anything happened...a break-in or...or something worse, it could be days before it was discovered.

"Stop it!" she said aloud. She was behaving like a neurotic old lady. Just because Adam had gone it didn't mean that the Blue Mountains were suddenly crawling with rapists.

"I thought that *pickney* would never go to sleep," said Penny, emerging from the bedroom and coming to sit at the other side of the desk. "These cards you makin' sure is pretty." She picked up the one titled "D is for duppy" and grinned. "Funny, too."

"I didn't want to scare Bram," Daisy explained, picking out a darker brown pencil for her illustration of an elephant's-ear seed pod.

"You could sell these, they so nice," Penny told her.

"These are for Bram," Daisy said. But it wasn't a bad idea. When she got home she'd think about that.

"Can I look at these?" asked Penny, indicating Daisy's portfolio, propped against the desk. Daisy nodded and Penny undid the tape and started going through the watercolours. "These is *irie*," she declared after a while. "I bet lots of people in Jamaica would like to buy these, jus' to show what ol' Gilbert did."

I wonder if the Disaster Fund Committee will be as keen, thought Daisy. Adam should be at the Hursts' now, showing them her paintings. She added some shading to the seed pod before saying casually, "Do you happen to know Adam's friend Amy?"

"Amy Preston? Sure! She come from an old Jamaican fambly."

Like the Deverells. A marriage between two old families, with plenty of money to sweeten the contract—no wonder Louise and Sheila were so keen.

"Is she nice?" Daisy went on, relentlessly probing.

"She's okay." Penny replaced the watercolours in the portfolio. "I jes' love your pictures, Daisy."

"Thank you." She laid aside her pencil. "And is Miss Preston pretty as well as rich?" It was like having a loose tooth. She couldn't let it alone.

"Yeah. She's pretty. Small an' dark."

Small and dark and wealthy—and championed by Sheila and Louise. That was quite a combination. Except—Adam didn't always do what his sisters wanted. And he didn't want to get married. Ever. So why was she feeling so threatened? So *jealous*. *Because let's face it,* she told herself. The sour lump in her throat was jealousy. Did it really matter to her if Adam married Amy Preston or... or anybody?

Yes. It did. And the sooner she came to terms with her feelings the better.

She put the cards together and snapped an elastic band around them. "That's it for tonight," she said to Penny. "I'm tired. I'm heading for bed."

Not to sleep though. She was far too tense to relax into sleep. She heard Bram whimper in the other room, and Penny started crooning to him. Then all was silent.

Daisy stood at her bedroom window. The rain had stopped earlier, and now moonlight gilded the trees. She leaned against the sill, feeling the soft breeze moving against her cheeks. From somewhere in the forest came the clear pipe of a nocturnal bird.

A deep sense of sadness flowed over Daisy. In less than two weeks she would be home, and this lush paradise would be nothing more than a memory. A portfolio full of evocative watercolours. And Adam? It was unlikely she would ever see him again. She had rebuffed him so often, why should he bother to look her up in England? No. They would go about their separate lives, and that would be that.

No, she thought, *I can't bear that!* And then she thought, *I love him. I love him desperately, and that's hopeless.*

She took a deep, shuddering breath and turned away from the illusory moonlight. It was good that she was going home. Getting away from him before she was in too deep.

But it didn't feel good, if felt like a small death.

CHAPTER TEN

EARLY MORNING WAS ALWAYS the loveliest time in the mountains, and soon after sunrise Daisy was out on the veranda sipping a mug of tea. The sky was a vast expanse of milky blue, not a cloud to be seen, and already the air felt warm. She folded back the sleeves of her kimono. It was going to be a scorcher.

After a restless night she had decided that she wasn't going to mope over Adam—well, not more than she could help. So she began planning the day's activities. Maybe a trip to the beach with Penny and Bram? A little holiday. It might help to take her mind off Adam.

She was about to go inside and rouse Penny when she heard a car coming up the road. Adam's Jeep drew up in front of the villa. Daisy's heart began to flutter.

"You're certainly the early bird," said Adam, jumping down from the Jeep.

She was so surprised and pleased to see him that all she could think to say was "You're early, too," which was hardly scintillating repartee. She'd have to do better than this if she wanted to captivate him and make him forget suitable women like Amy Preston. Not that she did, of course. Still, she didn't want to bore him.

When he came up the steps she pulled her kimono tighter and saw him glance involuntarily at the points of her nipples against the silk. "I remember that garment," he said gruffly.

And she remembered the uninhibited response of her body under it, and her cheeks grew warm.

He indicated the mug she was clutching. "Any tea left in the pot?"

"I think so. If there isn't I can soon make some fresh. Come inside." *Why am I inviting him in as if he's a stranger?* she thought. *He's been living with me for three weeks, in a manner of speaking, and here I am, behaving as if I've never laid eyes on him before.*

"Tea all right? Or would you rather have coffee?" She sounded so formal. So self-conscious. Well, that was the way she felt. She felt self-conscious. Aware that she had forced him to move, that she had hurt him.

"Have you had breakfast?" she asked, heading for the kitchen.

"I thought you'd never ask!" He grinned and handed her a paper bag. "I brought some eggs and some of Lilly's marmalade as a contribution."

"Oh, lovely! Thank you." She started babbling. "I could make omelets for us all. I make good omelets. Or do you think Bram would rather have his egg boiled? Children can be funny about food, can't they?"

"Most amusing." He lightly stroked a strand of her hair from her cheek and the touch of his fingers was like a small electric jolt. "Before Penny and the boy surface, don't you want to hear my news?"

For a crazy moment she thought he might be about to tell her that he had decided to marry Amy after all. She looked up at him, her hazel eyes anxious. "What news, Adam?"

"About your paintings, angel."

Relief flooded over her like spring rain. "Oh! The Disaster Fund. Did they like them?"

"Of course they did. The committee was delighted. The auction will make a lot of money for the island. But the best part of it is..."

"Yes?"

"You've got commissions for three paintings for some of the committee. I tell you, Daisy, they were knocked out by your talent. And once the general public sees your work at the dinner, the orders will be pouring in. I told them your fee," he added, and named a sum that made her head spin.

"But—but I can't paint three pictures in the time left here," she said.

"You don't have to. You can do them when you get home. You've got plenty of sketches."

"Y-yes." She blinked up at him, bemused.

This would solve a lot of her money problems. And she had Adam to thank for it. Her instinct was to throw her arms around him and kiss him. But she was shy with him this morning, so instead she mumbled, "Thank you, Adam," and started taking the eggs out of the bag.

"Now get a move on, angel," he urged. "Your first appointment's at nine."

"Appointment?"

"With one of your new clients. Wake *up*, Daisy! Mrs. Preston's a busy woman, we mustn't keep her waiting."

Preston! Daisy's sudden euphoria evaporated like mist in the sun. "Any relation of Amy's?"

"Her mother. Why?"

"Oh!" She got out mixing bowls and a fork. "Are you sure she wants one of my pictures?"

"Of course I'm sure." He sounded exasperated. "She was bowled over by your stuff."

"And what about Amy?"

"What about her?"

"Was she bowled over, too?"

"I don't know. She didn't say." He pushed his glasses up his nose. "But she didn't vote against the art sale."

"Goody for her!" She started viciously cracking eggs against the side of the bowl. *I must stop acting like this,* she thought. *I'm being childish.* But she couldn't seem to stop. "Does Amy know anything about art?" She picked up a fork and started beating the eggs.

"Let's just say she knows what she likes."

"One of those!"

"Well, if you meet her this morning you can educate her." He looked at her quizzically. "You're going to turn those eggs into leather, angel, if you go on like that."

She stopped taking her feelings out on the eggs and began setting the table.

"Shall I start on the omelets?" Adam inquired. "Or do you want to do it yourself?"

She said stiffly, "Go ahead. I can hear sounds from Penny's room. I expect they'll be out soon."

By the time Penny and Bram had surfaced and breakfast was on the table, Daisy had herself under control. But she was still startled at the ferocity of her emotions. She had never felt jealous before. She'd certainly never been jealous of Nigel, not even when he'd flirted with a particularly pretty teller at his bank. But in the three years she'd known him, he'd never aroused any extreme feelings in her. He'd never made her feel that if she lost him her heart would shrivel up like a walnut....

She gave herself a mental shake and pushed aside the rest of her omelet. *You can't lose what you've never had, Daisy. Pull yourself together!*

She took longer than usual getting ready because Adam made her change out of her neat linen skirt and jacket, into shorts and running shoes. She'd wanted to look her best in case she did meet Amy, but it seemed that he had plans, and high-heeled shoes and a tight skirt didn't fit into them.

"That's better," he said, eyeing her turquoise shorts and halter top appreciatively.

"It seems a bit casual for a business meeting," said Daisy, pulling on a yellow shirt as a cover-up.

"As we say in this country—*no problem!* Besides, you look good enough to eat."

And that's one in the eye to you, Amy Preston!
thought Daisy, putting her spit-box and a small jar of
water into her holdall.

They dropped off Penny and her son in Kingston,
after arranging to pick them up later. Daisy had felt
guilty, leaving her guests to fend for themselves, but
Penny had relatives in town, and she was delighted to
have a chance to visit them.

It was an hour's drive from Kingston to the Prestons' farm, through countryside lush with new growth.
Heat shimmered like water in the valleys, and hawks
hovered lazily on the sultry air currents. Daisy began
to relax. She was going to spend a whole day with
Adam, who seemed to have forgiven her for throwing
him out. That was one of the nice things about him,
she thought. He didn't bear grudges. Nigel would have
punished her for days.

"Things are beginning to look better," said Adam,
indicating an orange grove that appeared quite tidy,
despite a lot of missing trees. "It looks as if Jamaica
is slowly getting on its feet again."

"What about your coffee crop?"

He shook his head. "It's too early to tell for sure,
but I suspect it's a write-off."

Impulsively she put her hand on his arm. "I'm so
sorry, Adam."

"We'll survive, angel," he said, briefly covering her
hand with his own. "We have other crops, so it won't
hurt us too much. Save your sympathy for the small
farmers. They're the ones I worry about."

He would, too, and he'd do something about it. Something practical. Look what he'd done for Devil's Gully. That was one of the things she loved about him—his genuine concern for people.

They turned into a long driveway, flanked by fields dotted with grazing cattle. Closer to the house a groom passed them, leading a beautiful chestnut horse.

"Amy breeds horses," Adam told her. "Horses and Dobermans."

"Oh?" *Who cares?* she thought bitterly.

"She's won a lot of prizes. She's recognized internationally."

"That's nice."

They drew up in front of the large porticoed house. Three fierce-looking dogs, some of Amy's brood presumably, started barking hysterically. Daisy was relieved to see that they were chained.

"Shut up, you lunatics! Can't you see it's Adam?" yelled a female voice.

Standing in the doorway was a petite woman dressed in jodhpurs. Every muscle in Daisy's body tensed. "You must be Daisy," the little woman said, coming down the steps. She was very tanned and had short dark hair. She aimed a cuff at the dogs. "Be quiet, you morons!" The animals stopped barking and tried to lick her hands. "They're beautiful brutes, but *stupid*!" She smiled warmly. "I'm Amy Preston. Welcome to the Preston madhouse."

"How do you do?" said Daisy. She added, "I'm happy to meet you," because Amy's welcome sounded so genuine that it was very nearly true.

"Well, it's about time." Amy led them into a shadowy drawing room, cluttered with riding whips, dogs' baskets and innumerable pamphlets on breeding lines and pedigrees. "Adam's been going on about you for weeks. We've been agog."

Adam protested, "How you do exaggerate. I don't go on, as you so elegantly put it."

"Not as a general rule," Amy agreed, "but this time you did." She turned to Daisy. "Besotted is the word that comes to mind."

Daisy smiled weakly. She was feeling distinctly confused. She was also feeling discouraged. Amy was nice. She was very nice, and there didn't seem a reason in the world why Adam shouldn't eventually want to marry her.

"This place is a real tip," Amy said, looking around the room. She removed a saddle from one of the shabby armchairs. "Park yourself," she commanded, and Daisy did. Amy perched herself on the arm, and grinned down at her. "Now, where was I?"

"Talking rubbish," Adam said. "Where's your mother, Amy? She's the one we've come to see."

"She was in the kitchen the last time I saw her. Why don't you go and rout her out? I want to talk to Daisy."

"All right. But watch what you say. I'll be right back, angel," he said to Daisy. "Don't pay any attention to this madwoman."

"Get going!" Amy threw a book on worming at his retreating back. When he'd gone she smiled broadly at Daisy. "You've really knocked him off his perch," she said.

Daisy stared at her, hazel eyes wide. "I have?"

Amy nodded energetically. "You'd better believe it! I've known Adam all my life, and there have been lots of ladies in his, but he's never lost his heart to any of them before."

Lots of ladies! Lost his heart! What was she talking about? "But I thought..." said Daisy. "I mean...don't his sisters think that...that you and Adam..."

Amy let fly with an expletive. "Louise and Sheila can't tell a Maltese puppy from a mastiff! Just because Adam and I had a romantic interlude one summer they seem to think we're bonded for life!" She jumped to her feet. "And you needn't look like that, Daisy. It was a very innocent interlude. We were teenagers, for Pete's sake! We're ancient now. In our thirties. It was aeons ago! What Louise and Sheila *really* want—" she put her hands on her hips "—what they really want is the Preston land. Not that the Deverells need more land, for heaven's sake, but Adam's sisters are greedy."

"What about Adam's father?" asked Daisy. "Is he greedy?"

"Bless your little pointed head, Adam's father would give you his last nosebag of oats if you needed it! Adam takes after him, too." She flung herself down on a dog-chewed ottoman. "The girls take after their mother," she said darkly. "I never knew her, but my mother did, and she says she was a holy terror."

But Daisy wasn't listening. She didn't care about Adam's mother. She didn't care about anything anymore. Amy didn't realize it, but she had removed a giant weight from Daisy's heart, and all Daisy could hear was, *Besotted is the word that comes to mind*.

Adam returned with Mrs. Preston, and Daisy showed her the contents of her portfolio. Mrs. Preston was glowing in her praise, and ordered two pictures instead of one. But Daisy was in such a daze that she scarcely took it in.

Lots of ladies, but he's never lost his heart to any of them before. If that was true, then surely they would go on seeing each other in England? Now, perhaps saying goodbye to Jamaica wouldn't mean saying goodbye to Adam as well.

"Thank you, thank you!" Daisy said to Mrs. Preston, who looked rather startled by such excessive gratitude. "I'll get the pictures to you as quickly as I can, and thank you again."

"You said that before." Adam grinned. "And now we'd better be off. There's still lots to do this morning."

They left the Preston farm and spent the remainder of the morning visiting the two other members of the committee who wanted Daisy to paint pictures for them: a Colonel Braydon, who wanted one of the parade ground at Newcastle, "with a bit of the wall in it, m'dear, and some of the military crests," and a Mr. and Mrs. Saxe Morton, who wanted studies of flowers for their sitting room.

"And that's enough to be going on with," said Adam as they drove away from the Saxe Mortons' bungalow. "Now it's time for lunch."

They bought spicy patties, and something called *janga*, which turned out to be peppered shrimp, from a take-out shop, and a bunch of the smallest bananas Daisy had ever seen, from a local market, and ate them sitting under a palm tree.

"This is the life," she said happily, brushing crumbs off her fingers. "I loved those pasties."

"Patties, angel. You're not in Cornwall now."

She smiled. "You have a point. They don't go in for hot pepper to the same extent in Trebethwick Cove."

"So that's where you live, is it?"

For an instant she felt her guard come up. But that was foolish. That whole sordid business with the press was over. It was in the past. Besides, she loved Adam. There was no need to hide anything from him anymore.

"Adam," she began hesitantly, "there's something I—"

"I don't know Cornwall," he said, speaking at the same time. "Will you show it to me?"

She could feel happiness radiating from her heart like a tropical sun. "Yes. I'd love to. But there's something I—"

"Because I'll be going back to England myself soon. And Daisy—" he took her hand and held it in both of his "—I don't want to lose track of you. Not when it's taken me so long to find you."

She wondered if he could feel the pounding of her heart, feel her hand tremble. "I've been here all the time," she said.

"I seem to remember that we got off to a bad start." He lifted her hand and gently kissed it.

"Yes, but that was because—"

"It was because I'm a prize idiot, angel." He gave a snort of disbelief. "To think I nearly sent you away. When I think of what I nearly lost." He drew her into his arms and started kissing her forehead, her cheeks, her eyelids. "Daisy, oh, Daisy! I've been such a fool."

"I didn't tell you the truth at first," she tried to explain between kisses. "The reason I didn't want to go to a hotel..."

"It doesn't matter, angel."

"But Adam..."

"No, my love!" He kissed her mouth, and she stopped trying to speak, abandoning herself to delight.

When the kiss ended he put his arm around her shoulders and drew her toward him so that her head lay against the warmth of his chest. "I want to start afresh, angel," he said. "No explanations. No past history. But I must know one thing." He tilted her chin and looked intently into her eyes. "This man you were engaged to. Do you still care for him?"

"No, I don't. And I didn't come to Jamaica because I broke up with Nigel. Not really. That's what I want to tell you...."

He gave a sigh and hugged her close. "You don't have to tell me anything, angel. As long as you're not pining away for this chap, nothing else matters."

"I'm not doing that," she promised him. Even if she'd not met Adam, there would have been precious little pining. She didn't feel any bitterness toward Nigel, but she now saw that to have married him would have been an act of total folly.

"I've been doing a lot of thinking about you lately," Adam said, "and it's my observation that you're due for a bit of wooing."

She snuggled closer. "I wouldn't object."

"The old-fashioned kind, angel. I'm not going to drag you into bed."

She drew her finger down his cheek. "That's too bad!"

He raised his brows in mock reproof. "What a wicked girl! If you keep on being so nice to me I can't promise I won't drag into a bush."

She sat up. "You turned me down flat once," she reminded him.

"I know. And in retrospect, I'm glad I did, Daisy." He touched a strand of her glossy hair, winding it round his finger. "I must have sensed, even then, that I wanted more from you than a casual relationship. And that terrified me," he added with a rueful smile. "You know my views about commitment."

She was tempted to ask him if his views had changed. It sounded like it. But it didn't seem right to ask him until she'd told him about Peggy Matheson's allegation and the storm of publicity that had followed it. One couldn't build any sort of relationship without a firm base of trust, and you couldn't build that if one party was keeping something back. However, this was not the time for confidences. It would be taking unfair advantage to tell him while he was making gentle love to her.

"And now, sweetheart," he said, "much as I would like to spend the rest of the afternoon sitting here kissing you, I understand that it's part of the ritual of wooing for the gentleman to take his lady for a romantic stroll." He rose, dragging her with him. "On your feet!"

"My feet have gone to sleep," she protested, hanging on to him.

"Then what you need is a short walk in Cockpit Country. Come along, angel." He kissed her chastely on the forehead. "Otherwise I may not be able to continue this admirable self-control."

After walking along a deep ravine for a mile or two, they scrambled through a tangle of liana and convolvulus, over a barrier of sun-baked rocks and into a windless glade filled with trees, most of which had escaped the fury of the hurricane. Escarpments of limestone jutted through the trees, giving the place a closed-in, claustrophobic feeling.

"If this is your idea of a romantic stroll, remind me never to go on a real hike with you." Daisy chuckled. The heat was oppressive, and she had removed her shirt, which was now tied around her waist by its sleeves.

"You wanted trees." He wiped the sweat away from his eyes. His T-shirt was as wet as if he'd been swimming. "You must admit, the foliage here is still in pretty good shape."

She gazed around this lovely, ominous place and nodded. The glade ended in a wall of solid rock, and beyond that was an endless maze of gullies and hollows, each one as silent and forbidding as the last.

Hastily she drew some rough sketches in her book, plucked samples of leaves from plants and trees and made notes about the pale apple-green colour at the heart of the convolvulus, and the shades of some of the other plants she found growing here. Her notes and drawings were uncharacteristically hurried. She didn't want to linger. She felt threatened by this place.

Perhaps she'd spent too long in the mountains, but this airless cockpit oppressed her. Not usually fanciful, she could easily imagine it filled with inhospitable spirits—malignant, threatening.

She was thankful when they started on the trek back, but the miasma of the place seemed to go with them. To cling like cobwebs.

She wished they had not come here. They should have stayed in the sunshine, in the fresh air. This stifling valley, this sense of danger was, she was convinced, a portent of bad luck.

CHAPTER ELEVEN

THEY COLLECTED Penny and Bram, and then the four of them went on a modest shopping spree. Daisy bought a stuffed rabbit and a toy train for Bram, and some small gifts for friends back home, but she couldn't quite shake off that sense of impending doom.

"You all right, Daisy?" Adam asked.

She nodded brightly. "I'm tired, that's all."

"What do you say we treat this young man to some ice cream, and then I'll take you home? You can get a rest before I pick you up for dinner." He led them toward an ice cream parlor. "Okay?"

"Lovely," she said. And it was. Daisy had rarely been cosseted in her life. It made a welcome change.

After he'd ordered for them, he went off on a mysterious errand of his own, leaving Bram beaming at a double scoop of chocolate pistachio.

"Mr. Adam is real *irie*, treatin' Bram like this," said Penny, tucking a tissue into her son's collar. She looked over at Daisy. "But you don't look so happy. You mad at somethin'?"

"Mad? Heavens, no!" said Daisy, attacking her raisin rum float with what she hoped looked like a burst of good humour.

"I jes' wondered if you maybe would rather have Tamarind Cottage to yourself right now." She smiled knowingly. "Seein' how things are between you an' Mr. Adam...I guess Bram an' me...we could be in the way."

"If I want to be alone with Adam, there are plenty of other places for us to go," Daisy assured her. "If I'm quiet it's because Adam took me tramping through one of those cockpits this afternoon, and it's knocked me out."

Penny looked horrified. "Lawd have mercy! That place jes' plumb full of *duppies*."

"Oh, come on!" said Daisy, who wasn't in the mood for this kind of talk.

"I'm tellin' you, Daisy, that place full of dead Maroons. It's bad luck goin' there."

"Well, from what I hear the Maroons were brave people," Daisy replied stoutly. "I don't mind their ghosts."

"But they jes' might mind *you*," said her friend. "You wouldn't catch me goin' there."

"Well, I won't go there again," Daisy promised. "Look at Bram! I think he's trying to take a bath in his ice cream."

"What you doin', chile?" cried Penny, looking in dismay at her son, who seemed to be covered to the waist in chocolate pistachio. She whipped the remnants of the soggy cone away from him. Bram gave her a startled look, and let out a roar of indignation. "Stop that. You *nyam* enough already!" said his flustered mother, attempting to wipe his face.

Adam returned in the midst of this uproar. He was looking very pleased with himself, and even a screaming child covered in ice cream didn't seem to disturb him. "That's a good pair of lungs on your son, Penny," he remarked amiably.

"Don't encourage him," said Daisy. "It may not bother you, but it's not good for the ice cream trade."

"Nothing could bother me at the moment." Adam grinned. "I've just tracked down the impossible." He leaned toward her and hummed softly, "'Daisy, Daisy, give me your answer do.'" Bram screamed louder. "I don't need any competition, thank you," Adam said, taking the child from Penny and putting him on his shoulders. "Now, shut up, Bram, there's a good chap."

Bram hiccoughed twice, and then stopped crying. He wound his sticky little fingers in Adam's hair and started to bounce up and down. "Horsey, horsey!" he demanded.

"That's more like it!" said Adam. "Now, let's get this show on the road."

Daisy helped Penny bathe her son when they returned to the cottage, and then she had a lazy, warm bath herself. Cautiously she allowed herself to relax. This feeling of impending doom must simply be a guilty conscience. Because she did feel guilty, not telling Adam who she really was and how she came to be in Jamaica. She should have insisted that he listen to her this afternoon, not let him drive all thoughts of confession out of her mind with his kisses.

His kisses! Just *thinking* about them sent a thrill of pleasure from her toes to the crown of her head. *And that's no way to carry on,* she told herself sternly, pulling the plug and letting the water run out. *This evening you tell him everything. You can't keep on putting it off.*

But it turned out that they were having dinner with Trevor Stokes and his wife that evening, and somehow, telling Adam on the way there didn't seem a good idea. And when it was time to say good-night and they had parked outside Tamarind Cottage, he deflected her by taking a slender gold chain from his pocket and putting it around her neck.

"A memento of a perfect day, sweetheart," he whispered, lightly kissing the curve of her jaw.

"Oh, Adam!" She fingered the gold sand dollar that was suspended from the chain. She had not received many presents in her life, and she had to blink away sudden tears. "It's beautiful. I...I... Oh, thank you!"

He stroked her cheek. "It's to bring you good fortune, angel. Not that you need a talisman. Your talent will bring you all the good fortune you can use. This is for... for personal happiness."

"Thank you," she whispered again, brushing his lips with hers, and she felt his desire match her own as their kiss deepened.

"You'd better go in, angel," he said breathlessly. "My spirit's willing to behave like a gentleman, but the flesh is weak. Besides, making love in cars is not for us," and in a daze of happiness and unfulfilled passion she stumbled into the house, her secret still unspoken.

Unfortunately, this pattern established itself. She simply couldn't seem to find the right moment. She did try, but either something interrupted them, or Adam started to make love to her, and his kisses drove all her good intentions from her mind.

Finally she lost her nerve. She began to believe that fate was telling her to leave well enough alone, to wait a little longer. For in spite of her newfound happiness she was still cautious.

Wasn't she, perhaps, being complacent, assuming Adam would offer her instant understanding? Nigel hadn't understood. Wouldn't she be taking a terrible risk? She had so much more to lose now. The emotion she'd felt for Nigel was insipid compared to the way she felt about Adam, but even so, it had hurt her terribly when Nigel refused to take her word. How much worse it would be if the same thing happened again. She would be devastated if Adam turned from her, or looked at her with his eyes full of doubt.

And so the days fled by, and Daisy kept putting off her confession. She would usually spend the afternoon with Adam at his beach house, painting and watching the troop of workmen clear the grounds that had been laid waste by the hurricane. Later in the day she and Adam would swim in the unbelievably blue waters, and lie under the shade of a thatched shelter to dry off.

In spite of standing in a wrecked garden the beach house was gorgeous. Built on a headland, it commanded a view of the sea from all its great windows, which captured every breeze and cooled the large white rooms even on the hottest days. At midday the maid would close the outside shutters, and the rooms would become a shadowy haven from the heat.

Adam had had to refurnish the house after the hurricane, and the light blues and apple greens he'd chosen complemented the white and coral of the rugs, which had been stored in high closets and had escaped the rainwater that had flooded in after the storm.

Daisy instantly fell in love with this house, and was very impressed to discover that Adam had designed it. "Surely there's a market for beautiful houses like this in the islands," she said.

"There is," he agreed. "I've designed a couple already, as a matter of fact, and I hope to get more commissions when I move back to Jamaica."

She sat upright in the green-striped lounger. "I thought ... I thought you said you'd never move back."

He poured a glass of pineapple juice from the jug on the table and handed it to her before replying. "That's what my sisters assume, but Dad and I agreed long ago that when he felt he was getting too old to manage the farms by himself, I'd come back and help him."

"I can understand you wanting to come back here," she said. But she was thinking mournfully, *He's leaving England! I'll never see him again.*

"Can you, angel?" He reached for his dark glasses. "You've really taken to Jamaica then?"

"It's stunning. Like a dream." She took a sip of her drink before saying in an offhand way, "What about your architectural business in England? Will you give it up?"

"Not entirely. I'll let my partner run it, and I'll work on getting a branch of the firm established here."

"Oh. You'll have time for that as well, will you?"

He gave her his lopsided grin, the one that always made her heart turn over. "Well, I won't be running the farms single-handed, Daisy. We do have staff."

"Of course." She'd forgotten for the moment that being a Deverell meant being wealthy.

"I shall still travel. Being an architect entails a fair bit of travelling."

"It sounds wonderful. A perfect life," she said with a brittle smile.

"It could be." He reached for the bottle of sunscreen lotion. "Let me put some of this on your shoulders, angel," he said. "We don't want you getting a burn." She stopped trying to figure out what he was trying to say and gave herself up to the delight of feeling his hands stroking the lotion into her skin.

From then until the last day of her stay they skirted around things. Adam would make oblique references about his return to Jamaica, but she would never press him for dates. She assumed that once he moved back she would rarely, if ever, see him again; knowing when the loneliness would start wouldn't ease the pain, so she kept off the subject. And she never got around to telling him her secret, either. If he was going to glide out of her life there no longer seemed to be any point. Safer by far to keep the memory of these last days together untarnished, so that it would be bright and unspoiled in the dreary days ahead.

Because of all these evasions her last week was not as carefree as it could have been. She found herself being cautious in conversation, being careful not to say anything that might be construed as some sort of promise to meet in England. For although they'd exchanged addresses, Adam had not said anything definite about seeing her over there, and Daisy was too proud to beg.

But, oh, she wanted to! The thought of taking up her life again without him around was like a knife in her heart. A sharp, cruel knife that she knew would get sharper as the time to say goodbye approached.

As the days rushed on Adam grew unusually quiet, and she wondered if he was getting tired of her company. *Dear God, please don't let him be bored by me,* she prayed. *I couldn't bear that.* As an antidote she tried repeating to herself all the nice things that Amy had said. But it didn't help. After all, Amy wasn't infallible. And even if Adam had once given the impression that he was "besotted," men got over that kind of thing. Look at Nigel! Look at her father!

She took to stealing furtive glances at him through the thick fringe of her lashes, and more than once she had caught him gazing at her speculatively over the top of his glasses. But if anything was bothering him he didn't tell her, and she felt it prudent not to ask.

The last day of her visit rolled around. She had hoped that Adam would spend the entire day with her instead of working on his beach house until it was time for their afternoon swim. But in spite of her imminent departure, it seemed that he was not about to change his routine. Another indication, she thought glumly, of his loss of interest.

She did most of her packing first thing in the morning. Her flight wasn't until early the next day, but she didn't want to leave things to the last minute; besides, she needed to be busy to keep depression at bay.

Penny gave her a hand, and Daisy, pretending that she was tired of several of her dresses, insisted that her friend accept them. "We get so little summer weather," she said. "I hardly ever wear them."

"Is it always winter in England?" asked Penny, holding up a yellow sundress.

"Some years it feels like it," Daisy replied. Without Adam in her life it would always feel like it, she thought, and the stone that seemed to have replaced her heart grew heavier.

Penny wanted to see how things were progressing with her roof, and so Daisy dropped her and Bram off at Devil's Gully and went in search of material for some last sketches.

She found several scissortailed hummingbirds whirring among the bright flowers of a hibiscus, and did a series of quick drawings. Adam had told her that these birds were called doctor birds by the local people, because the black crest on their minute heads recalled the days when doctors wore top hats. She added a hat and a doctor's bag to one of the sketches. She'd give that one to Bram as a parting gift.

It was a blazing hot day, but the forest was still and shadowy. Occasionally the silence was broken by the rustle of a foraging bird. A yellowback finch perched on a nearby tree. The mountains had never been lovelier.

Her work blurred in front of her eyes, and Daisy, blinking away tears, closed her sketchbook with a slap, sending off the finch with a scutter of wings.

Tomorrow this magical place would be just a memory. And Adam...Adam would be a memory, too, for by now she had convinced herself that he didn't intend to continue the friendship.

And the worst thing, she realized, would be the knowledge that she'd never been honest with him. Never trusted him enough to tell him the truth. What would he think of her if he ever found out? He'd *despise* her. And he'd take her silence as an admission of guilt. She wouldn't be there to explain. And even if she was, what difference would it make? By her remaining silent the damage was done.

She'd been an idiot. A spineless idiot. But maybe she could still make it come right. Well, perhaps not right, but—better. There was still time to tell him.

"That's what I'll do!" she said aloud, jamming her sketchbook into her pack. The hummingbirds flew to the other side of the bush. She wouldn't wait until the afternoon. She'd go down to the beach house *now* and tell him everything. Even if he was angry with her it would be better than this awful suspense, this sense of treacherousness. And if he never wanted to see her again, if she had to spend her last evening in Jamaica alone and unhappy, she would at least be free of the deceit. It would be a clean pain.

When she drew up at the beach house she was so overwrought that she didn't notice the estate car parked among the worker's trucks. The front door was open and she went in, intending to go through the house into the garden, which was where Adam spent most of his time.

The door to the living room was ajar, and as she put her hand on the knob to push it open she became aware of someone talking, and recognized Louise's strident tone.

Daisy froze, her hand still stretched for the doorknob.

"I'm telling you, Adam, the girl's *notorious*," Louise was saying. "Read the article if you don't believe me. She's out to make a fool of you—and you're falling for it."

Adam said something then, but he spoke so softly Daisy couldn't make out the words. Whatever he said, it made Louise's voice rise a decibel.

"I don't know what's come over you. You never used to be such a fool over a pretty face. Introducing her to our friends. Getting them to buy her wretched paintings. That's what she wants, you know. To get herself established in a wealthy set and bleed you dry in the process."

"I'm giving you one minute to get out, Louise," Adam said savagely.

"She's no good, Adam," Louise railed. "She's a liar. She didn't even tell you her real name. *Daisy!*" she derided. "It sounds like a comic song."

"That will do!" Adam thundered. "You have no proof that this Marguerite Gordon and Daisy are the same person, and until I've spoken to her I refuse to discuss it."

Daisy couldn't stand it another moment. With a crash she flung open the door. Louise and Adam, who had been facing each other, both whirled around in surprise. Adam was holding the magazine that contained the incriminating "Marguerite, Where Are You?" article, and Daisy's photograph stared accusingly at her.

"It's true," she said. "I'm Marguerite Gordon."

"You see!" Louise cried in triumph.

"I should have told you before," she said to Adam, "but ... but now you know ..." Oh! if only Louise hadn't been there, she could have talked to him honestly. But his sister's expression of triumph made Daisy tongue-tied. Besides, she was damned if she was going to start explaining things in front of this gloating enemy.

"I'll ... I'll say goodbye now," she said, head high. "I think that's best, don't you?"

With an oath Adam started toward her, but she eluded him. "Thank you for everything, Adam," she said, and then she turned and ran quickly from the room before he had a chance to grab her.

As she started the car she caught sight of Adam coming out onto the front step. She heard him call, "Daisy!" but she slammed the car into gear and raced out of the driveway at top speed.

She didn't want any postmortems. Not now. What was the point? The worst had happened, and it was her own fault. Her silence made all Louise's accusations appear just. There was nothing left for her to do now but go away.

The dusty road ahead misted in a shimmer of tears and she blinked and slowed down. She didn't need an accident on top of everything else.

It was then that Adam's Jeep came into view in her rearview mirror. He passed her, going like a bat out of hell, and skidded to a stop, barring her way, forcing her to halt at the side of the road.

He came over and wrenched her door open, pulling her out of her car.

What was he planning to do? Beat her up? No! Not Adam. Just the same she felt a frisson of fear and ineffectually tried to free herself from his iron grasp. He dragged her to the Jeep and snarled, "Get in!"

"Adam...please..."

"Don't argue, dammit! Get in the bloody Jeep."

"Wh-where are we going?" she faltered.

"Back to the beach house—" he pushed her unceremoniously into the passenger seat "—to talk."

"No! Not with Louise there," she cried.

Adam gave his opinion of his sister in a carefully chosen expletive. "She's gone," he added grimly. "I threw her out."

"Just the same..."

He vaulted up beside her, slewed the Jeep around and proceeded to drive back at breakneck speed.

"Look, I can understand you being angry," Daisy said, hanging on with both hands, "but no amount of talking about it is going to make it better."

"Shut up!"

"But—"

"Shut *up*," he snarled so fiercely she didn't dare say another word.

Within moments they had swung into his driveway, and he switched off the engine. The steady pounding of the surf filled the abrupt silence.

"Don't you ever—*ever*—do that again," he said.

"Do what?" Lie? Get herself written about in the newspapers?

"Don't ever run away from me again, Daisy. I can't . . ." He glared at her. "You mustn't run away."

"I didn't think of it as running away." She gulped. "I thought of it more as . . . as getting away. I didn't think you'd want me around anymore. Not now that you know . . . about me. Who I really am."

"I know who you really are, Daisy," he said gruffly.

She stared up at him, surprised. "You know? About the scandal? The newspaper stories?"

"Oh, that! I don't give a twopenny fig about that." He pushed his hands through his hair, dislodging his glasses in the process. "Is it true?"

"It's not, as a matter of fact," she replied wearily.

"Then forget it," he said. "It's not important."

"Not important!" She could have hit him. "It just about ruined my life, that's all."

"Why didn't you tell me about it? I would have understood."

"I know that now, but I didn't then. And later on . . . when we became friends, well, I was afraid you wouldn't believe me."

"Of course I believe you," he declared.

"Well, you'd be the first," she returned. "I'm not used to having my word taken automatically, anymore."

"Well, you'd better get used to it again," he barked. "Anyone with half a mind could tell that you're no liar. Now you come with me!" He leaped out of the Jeep and started pulling her toward the garage. "I want to show you something."

"Adam, what are you doing?" she protested, sick of being dragged about like a sack of coffee beans.

"Look!" he said, throwing open the garage door.

The garage was empty, except for a couple of ladders stacked against one wall, and a tandem bicycle standing on a spread tarpaulin. It had just been given a fresh coat of bright pink paint, and gleamed gaudily in the muted sunshine.

Mystified, she shook her head. "A bicycle! I don't understand."

Adam pushed his glasses up his nose. "A bicycle built for *two*."

"Yes...but..."

"It was my surprise. I was going to ride it down to the beach this afternoon...in order to ask you..." He swallowed hard. "To ask you to marry me."

A proposal—from *Adam*—not possible! "But you hate marriage."

He looked at her, his face haggard. "I've changed my mind. Oh, Daisy, I love you so much. I need you more than peace, or comfort, or life." He lifted her hands and held them, palms upward. "Without you I'm nothing."

She stared at him, huge eyes luminous. "I thought you were losing interest in me."

"Angel! No!"

"Men do. Nigel did. And my father."

He pressed her palms together, and crushed her hands in his. "I'm not Nigel. Nor am I your father. I'm Adam Deverell, and I'm imploring you to marry me. If you turn me down I shall come to Cornwall—with my bicycle—and ask you again and again, until you say yes."

She started to laugh, and then because she'd been living so close to the edge, she started to cry, and he pulled her into his arms and kissed her face, her hair, her lips.

"Will you marry me? Will you, angel?" he murmured between kisses.

"Yes. Oh yes, Adam!" she gasped. "Only—I really did think you'd gone off me." She stared up at him, her lashes still starred with tears. "You haven't been very demonstrative lately."

"Oh, my darling!" He smoothed away a tendril of hair that was clinging to her damp cheeks. "I've never loved any woman the way I love you. I knew that if I kissed you or touched you, I wouldn't be able to stop. And I didn't want you thinking that asking you to marry me was a trick to get you into bed. So I held back." He tilted her chin, and looked at her with eyes glowing with love. "I was scared too, angel. I'd made such a song and dance about my aversion to matrimony, I was afraid you wouldn't take me seriously. Then I got the idea of using the bike as a...a sort of prop. If I kept everything light...made a sort of joke about it...I thought you might be disarmed enough to say 'yes.' I couldn't believe my luck when I found a secondhand tandem my first try...."

"The day we took Penny and Bram for ice cream!" she said, remembering his buoyant mood that afternoon.

"The very same. I thought it was a good omen. But when you threw me out of the villa—"

She protested, "I didn't *throw* you..."

"Not literally, angel, but it shook my self-confidence, I can tell you. You were right to get Penny in, of course." He smiled wryly. "I was going pretty short on sleep, apart from everything else, knowing you were lying in the next room."

He hugged her close and she could feel the thudding of his heart beating in rhythm with her own. "I only did it because I knew I couldn't keep on saying no, but I couldn't bear to have a casual affair with you," she said, hugging him tighter. "It would have broken my heart, Adam."

When he'd kissed her hard, to prove that casual was the last thing he felt about her, she said, "Your sisters won't be very happy about this. Particularly now that they know who I am. Know all the gossip about me."

He held her slightly away from him. "My choice of a wife has nothing to do with my sisters."

"Just the same," she insisted, "they're bound to think it's a comedown. Their brother marrying a gardener's daughter."

"What about you? An artist marrying a farmer's son?" He gave her a little shake. "Don't be a snob, angel. Besides, I know my sisters. In a year they'll be convinced the whole thing was their idea. And wait till you're famous! They'll take full credit!"

"You're convinced I'm going to become famous, are you?" She grinned.

"If you want to be. It's up to you, angel. You have the talent, and you know I'll support you all the way."

"Darling Adam," she said. Then she gave a yelp. "Oh Lord! I'm leaving you tomorrow. I'd forgotten."

He shook his head and his dark hair fell untidily across his forehead. "No way, angel. I'm coming with you. I've had my ticket for ages."

"Oh, Adam! Adam." She felt dazed with so much happiness.

He removed his glasses and carefully put them into his pocket, then he kissed her again in earnest.

"Don't you think we've admired the bicycle long enough? Let's go into the house," he said, his voice as soft as the mountain mist. "It's more comfortable than the garage."

MUCH LATER DAISY SAID, "Do you know what I'm going to do when we get to England?" She burrowed happily against his chest. "I'm going to write a thank-you note to Peggy Matheson. If it hadn't been for her I would never have come to Jamaica."

"We'll send flowers," said Adam. And then he started kissing her again.

From *New York Times* Bestselling author
Penny Jordan, a compelling novel of ruthless passion
that will mesmerize readers everywhere!

Penny Jordan

Silver

Real power, true power came from
Rothwell. And Charles vowed to have it,
the earldom and all that went with it.

Silver vowed to destroy Charles, just as surely and
uncaringly as he had destroyed her father; just as he had
intended to destroy her. She needed him to want her . . .
to desire her . . . until he'd do anything to have her.

But first she needed a tutor: a man who wanted no one.
He would help her bait the trap.

Played out on a glittering international stage,
Silver's story leads her from the luxurious comfort of
British aristocracy into the depths of adventure,
passion and danger.

AVAILABLE NOW!

HARLEQUIN

Harlequin Presents...

PENNY JORDAN

a rekindled passion

Over twenty years ago, Kate had a holiday
affair with Joss Bennett and found herself
pregnant as a result. Believing that Joss had
abandoned her to return to his wife and child,
Kate had her daughter and made no attempt
to track Joss down.

At her daughter's wedding, Kate suddenly
confronts the past in the shape of the
bridegroom's distant relative—Joss. He quickly
realises that Sophy must be his daughter and
wonders why Kate never contacted him.

Can love be rekindled after twenty years?
Be sure not to miss this AWARD OF EXCELLENCE
title, available wherever Harlequin books
are sold.

Take 4 bestselling love stories FREE

Plus get a FREE surprise gift!

What do *you* want for Christmas?

Jillian in SILVER BELLS wants a safe,
conventional husband.

Holly in DECK THE HALLS wants success.

But what you wish for isn't always
what you get.
Sometimes what you get is much
much better.

Join Holly and Jillian as they discover that
Christmas is a time for
romance . . . Harlequin® romance.

Don't miss
these special Christmas Romances
coming in:

#3091 DECK THE HALLS
by Heather Allison
#3092 SILVER BELLS
by Val Daniels

DEC-1

Win 1 of 10 Romantic Vacations and Earn Valuable Travel Coupons Worth up to $1,000!

Inside every Harlequin or Silhouette book during September, October and November, you will find a PASSPORT TO ROMANCE that could take you around the world.

By sending us the official entry form available at your favorite retail store, you will automatically be entered in the PASSPORT TO ROMANCE sweepstakes, which could win you a star-studded London Show Tour, a Carribean Cruise, a fabulous tour of France, a sun-drenched visit to Hawaii, a Mediterranean Cruise or a wander through Britain's historical castles. The more entry forms you send in, the better your chances of winning!

In addition to your chances of winning a fabulous vacation for two, valuable travel discounts on hotels, cruises, car rentals and restaurants can be yours by submitting an offer certificate (available at retail stores) properly completed with proofs-of-purchase from any specially marked PASSPORT TO ROMANCE Harlequin® or Silhouette® book. The more proofs-of-purchase you collect, the higher the value of travel coupons received!

For details on your PASSPORT TO ROMANCE, look for information at your favorite retail store or send a self-addressed stamped envelope to:

PASSPORT TO ROMANCE
P.O. Box 621
Fort Erie, Ontario L2A 5X3

-- ✂

 ONE PROOF-OF-PURCHASE   3-CHR-3

To collect your free coupon booklet you must include the necessary number of proofs-of-purchase with a properly completed offer certificate available in retail stores or from the above address.